there'll be scary ghost stories

AN INKWELLS & ANVILS ANTHOLOGY

INKWELLS & ANVILS

First Published by Inkwells & Anvils 2024

Cover Design by E.P. Fuselier

Compiled & Formatted by Catherine Stewart

Edited by Grace Malinee, Ben Stapleton, Kelly Gross, E.P. Fuselier, & Paige Guerra

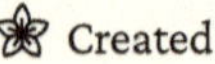 Created with Vellum

contents

*For all the Catholic Storytellers who have gone before us,
in thanksgiving for their example & intercession*

CATHERINE STEWART

St. Francis de Sales once said, "Be who you are and be that well." I take to heart with all I do, particularly when it comes to who I am as an artist. For, as Pope St. John Paul the Second reminds us, all artists —storytellers included—are 'ingenious creators of beauty' and are called to make masterpieces of our lives. In this anthology, not only are there masterpieces of stories, but each one was written by an author who wrote what they write, and wrote that well.

I think it fitting that Inkwells & Anvils' [I&A] first book is not one that is the result of a single mind, or even a single story, but a collection of stories from authors near and far. After all, I&A is a community of Catholic storytellers. Together we believe in the power of words and our common calling to pursue the perfection we are made for in Christ. It's a thrill to see just how we pursue that perfection together, whether it be in monthly challenges, in silly discourse, or in the trenches of the storytelling world where we are battered and only kept aloft by the knowledge that we're not alone.

So when we at I&A considered what we wanted to do for our first ever anthology, the idea of reaching for those kinds of stories told around fires in the cold struck a chord in our hearts. A return to a lost tradition that brought people—families, friends, groups—together for the passing of time by the sharing of stories. Not just any stories, but ones that left chills down the spine and reminded people of death, grief, the unknown, and above all, hope. Hope which outlasts the cold, which outlasts despair, and which keeps us doing what we do as we trust in the promises of Christ.

I don't think there is one single story that could show what it means to be part of a Catholic storyteller's community, and the hope it brings, but nine stories can give you a good look at the incredible variety of ways in which we respond to the inspiration we receive. Inspiration that calls us to remember the transcendentals: that which is good, that which is true, and that which is beautiful.

May these nine tales from ingenious writers of beauty and explorers of truth remind you of the hope that I see, and we as a community know, to be eternal.

Merry Christmas to all, and to all a good *write*.

Catherine Stewart, Inkwells & Anvils Co-Founder, Anthology Contest Compiler & Organizer

the examination of esther

JESSICA MCKENDRY

IT WAS CHRISTMAS EVE, and Arabella Aberdeen was confined to bed with a cold. It was a wretched sort of cold, much given to thievery, having already stolen Arabella's voice as well as the ability to breathe through her left nostril. Her misery was only added to by the fact that she and her family were spending Christmas at Oxenhoath Manor on the invitation of Arabella's uncle, and everyone else was having a very jolly week, while she manifestly was not.

The rest of the household had departed for Midnight Mass — all save the footman in the vestibule, whose scepticism prevented his having faith in anything other than newspaper articles and cold beef pie.

Upstairs, Arabella lay with the covers drawn up to her nose, and her head swathed in a voluminous tartan scarf. A squat cast-iron radiator did its best to warm the grand expanse of the second-best guest room. Somewhere above her stretched a high, vaulted roof, lost in the dormant dark.

Arabella regretted snuffing out her candle. Even a light under the door would have been something. Though she had only to stick her hand past the bedpost and feel about for a bellpull that would summon a light, she hesitated. She had read a set of lurid tales over the holidays, and now her fertile imagination suggested any number of vaguely unpleasant things that might lie in the sleeping darkness, just beyond the perimeter of the bed, ready to snap at a young maiden's tender fingers...

Arabella tucked a hot water bottle more securely under her arm, and let her feet burrow deeper into their blanket cocoon.

A grandfather clock stood watch over the door, an unsleeping sentinel. The clock hands moved in their eternal circle with sedate, deliberate care, moment to moment, minute to minute, just as they had done for the last sixty odd years. The pendulum sounded each beat in its casket — (*tick... tock...*) — buried behind the wood like the tell-tale heart.

Abruptly, the room became very cold — cold as an icebox. The air burned raw and chill against Arabella's nose. Into that empty, frozen dark came a noise: barely there, barely a scrape across the floorboards. It intruded on her senses — a thing that shouldn't be there, but it *was*. It came with faint, furtive tread, like a graverobber slinking into a crypt.

It arrived at the end of her bed, a footfall near the bedpost, and there it halted. Arabella shrank beneath the covers. Her hands were pressed tightly over her ears. She took a deep breath. She hoped the the— the *something* would be gone when she listened again.

When she finally dared to lower her hands, the room was quiet and warm again. The steady ticking of the grandfather clock came through the stillness. Arabella reached up to the high collar of her nightgown and undid the top button, loosening it about her throat. She swallowed. Her heart flubbered in her chest — a jarring, unpleasant sensation, worse than the time she fell down a staircase in the dark.

There was a faint smell of burning feathers. It tickled the girl's nose. She felt a sneezing fit approaching: she held the first sneeze in, but the second caught her off-guard and flew out with a violent *atchoo*. Groaning, Arabella fell back on her pillow and reached into her lace-covered sleeve for a hanky.

After the nasty business of blowing her nose and clearing her tired throat, Arabella lay there wondering if she ought to ring for the footman to bring her a light. Perhaps she could read a book. She sat up and stretched out her hand for the bellpull near the bedpost. Her fingertips touched the cord; a chill ran prickling down her arm, as if she'd brushed against a frost-coated window.

Arabella jerked the bellpull. Distantly in the corridor beyond rang the bell. After a time, a set of ponderous footsteps approached the bedroom door. It was the solid, shambling gait of a man who had been drawn up two flights of stairs with great reluctance, leaving behind him a snug fireside seat, a newspaper, and a tankard of mulled wine; and Arabella felt unexpectedly cheered by it.

The door creaked open, and the footman looked in. The golden light of a candle shone along the creases in his jowl and the ridges of his cheeks.

"You rang, miss? I trust all is well."

Arabella waved her hand, beckoning him forward. The footman's chest puffed up in a large, silent sigh of displeasure at being made to enter the room. He walked over to the foot of the bed and lifted his dark, caterpillar-furred eyebrows expectantly.

Arabella coughed, and then said, in a whisper as loud as a mouse's shout and as quiet as a startled raindrop: "Mister Morris, would you bring me a light?"

(Her voice was hardly present — indeed little more than a rasp remained, the rest having been purloined, as I mentioned, by the cold.)

The footman — rightfully addressed as Morris — went over to a candlestick sitting on a nightstand and lit it from the tallow candle in his own hand.

He turned about and said, curtly, "Anything else, miss?"

Arabella glanced around at the far reaches of the room, at the corners still deep in shadow beyond the halo of candlelight. She sank lower into the pillows, till her chin was tucked up against the bedcovers.

"Well..." she managed to get out, her voice as creaky as a weathervane in a gale, "I did... *hear* something." She cast her eyes up, bright with traces of fever.

The footman's mouth twitched as he looked at his young charge, and said, in a bored tone, "Has the ghost been bothering you?"

Arabella's eyes went wide, demanding explanation.

Morris put a closed fist to his mouth and coughed lugubriously into his knuckles. "The ghost of Oxenhoath manor, miss. As the tale goes, a young lass — possibly your age, if you'll pardon me — worked here as a lady's maid. She had the misfortune to fall in with one of the gardeners, to the dismay of her family and most particularly her mistress. The mistress took her maid to Europe, hoping to break the attachment. But the maid discovered the ploy. She fled at night, and was next seen at Calais, begging for a boat to Dover. Alas, she was cast upon by brigands, and though 'tis said she fought gallantly, they robbed her and left her for dead. The captain of a merchant vessel found her lying on the docks. He wept when he told the story, for her face was beautiful as an angel, but her eyes had been cut to pieces, and he knew she was not long for this world. Surgeons worked through the night, but in the end, they could not save her."

His eyelids drooped low, reducing his eyes to a narrow glimmer beneath the shadow of his brow.

"They buried her in her favourite spot, 'neath the lavender and rosemary bushes in the garden. It is rumoured that she roams once a year, on the night that she perished so tragically — a sightless spectre, overturning furniture and snuffing out candles, still raging at the misfortunes that led to her demise." At the conclusion of his speech, Mr. Morris folded his hands and shut his eyes, as if briefly overcome.

"Is it true?" Arabella dared to whisper at last.

"Upon my soul it is," intoned Morris. "Other guests have also reported disturbances of that nature in this very room on Christmas Eve."

(As mentioned at the beginning of this story, Mr. Morris was a sceptic of the first water. We must not do our noble footman the injustice of supposing him a traitor to his principles. His calm conviction in the ghost's existence did not extend to all ghosts in general — nay — only to this particular ghost, and only because he had read the entire story in the newspaper, and henceforth regarded the manor hauntings as a quaint and harmless reality of life.)

Mr. Morris wished her a cordial 'good night', and left the room with calm, unbothered tread. The door shut behind him with a gentle click.

Arabella picked up a book from the nightstand. She paused to look at the cover, embossed in gold. The red clothbound cover was stamped with an illustration of a seemingly empty smoking jacket seated upright in a wicker chair. One hollow sleeve raised a glass of gin to an unseen mouth, while near the jacket hem, a pair of slippers swayed lazily to and fro. It was H.G. Wells' *The Invisible Man*. Hardly the best reading material, under the circumstances, but nonetheless Arabella began valiantly on the second chapter, where she had left off earlier.

She had just reached the passage where the innkeeper's wife enters upon the stranger's room unexpectedly and sees something she should have not—

But for a second it seemed to her that the man she looked at had an enormous mouth wide open—a vast and incredible mouth that swallowed the whole of the lower portion of his face. It was the sensation of a moment: the white-bound head, the monstrous goggle eyes, and this huge yawn below it...

Arabella shivered. Ordinarily, she liked having her blood curdled by this sort of thing, especially in the company of the other girls back at school. But tonight was different. Tonight...

Arabella froze, book held aloft. The room was no longer quiet. The noises had started again. They were further off this time: little hints of movement about the room, footsteps soft as coal falling into the coal scuttle. There was a phonograph to one side of the room, and the footsteps seemed to be moving towards it.

She could see nothing in the faint gloom beyond the candlelight, but to her ears came the metal *clunk* of a wax cylinder being slotted into the phonograph. There was the sound of the crank winding, then a rustling, grainy crackle as the needle bit the wax.

A stentorian voice boomed to all corners of the room, *"God Rest You Merry Gentlemen, by The Meister Glee Singers."* Arabella let out a croak of fright. A brass band sprang into being, and a chorus of male voices trumpeted out, *"God rest you merry gentlemen, let nothing you dismay!"*

She pulled the covers over her head. *The Invisible Man* tumbled off the bed and landed with a clap on the floor, pages all awry.

"For Jesus Christ our saviour was born on Christmas day," the choristers warbled gaily, while Arabella lay as still as a frightened rabbit and breathed hotly through the cotton sheet with terror in her heart.

The music clanged on, drowning out any sound or sign that might warn her of a ghost approaching. Arabella pictured the shadow of a hand descending, grasping the blankets, tearing them away. Who ever said blankets were proof against a preternatural entity, anyway? She was no safer (she reasoned) beneath its gently sinking folds than above them.

For a moment, she thought that perhaps, since it was a lady ghost, it wouldn't do anything nasty. But then Arabella remembered how spiteful the girls at school could be, and how vengeful were the spirits of ladies crossed in love (she had read enough Mary Elizabeth Braddon for *that*), and her heart sank.

The footman wouldn't come to her rescue, she knew, not if she were plagued by all the ghosts in England — his advice had been to "pay no heed to it", just as he might tell someone to ignore the scullery maids having a brawl in the larder, or the dogs yapping after the milk cart.

She swallowed and snuffled. Only two options remained, then: to sit tight and wait things out, or to leave the room, hoping, in either case, that with the stroke of midnight and the arrival of Christmas, the otherworldly presence in her bedroom would vanish.

"—tidings of comfort and joy—"

The carol finished on a long, blaring note, and then stopped. Arabella harkened intently for any noises from the ghost. Several minutes passed. Slowly, the girl rose from the covers. Her hair was sticking out like the wires on a chimney brush. She put up her hands and distractedly smoothed it down.

At her bedside, the flame of the candle held steady in its pool of molten wax, nibbling at the wick. What had the footman said, that the ghost snuffed out candles when it passed? The candle was burning strong, so perhaps the ghost had gone.

Arabella bit her lip. Waiting here was a grisly prospect, even by candlelight. Grislier still was the idea of *leaving* the bed and making for the door. But Arabella had that indefinable thing known as "pluck" (an essential ingredient to surviving unwanted nightly visitations from ghosts and burglars and similar nuisances).

Her feet emerged from beneath the covers. She dangled them over the edge of the mattress and surveyed the distance between her bed and the door. Rallying her spirits, Arabella got down from the bed. Carefully, she picked up the candlestick. She lifted her nose bravely into the air and tiptoed for the door.

Her dress swept against her legs in a rush of freezing cold wind. The candle went out. The world dropped black around her like the curtain-fall on Judgement Day.

Arabella dove to the floor. Hot wax spilled from the candle, onto her hand. She clenched her fists and pressed her forehead to the floor. The wooden boards were smooth and cold against her skin.

She did not scream; she did not cry. She stayed as quiet as she possibly could, and prayed they wouldn't find her dead in the morning. A handful of soft, small things fell into her hair, tumbled against her cheek. She smelled lavender and rosemary. Close to her ear came a coaxing whisper — "Miss Aberdeen!"

Ripples of terror went down the girl's back. It spurred Arabella to move again, crawling to the door on trembling knees. Her fingers dug into the floorboard cracks as if to pull herself along faster.

A photograph fell from the wall by the door. It crashed against the floor, then toppled with a wail of breaking glass.

Suddenly, the bed seemed a far safer place. Arabella turned on her tail and scrabbled back to her bed. Her nightgown dragged behind her, spread across the floorboards like a winding sheet. The lace edge caught on a splinter; she whimpered and jerked it free.

She bumped into the bedhead. Stars of pain flashed before her eyes, and her teeth chattered. Too dizzy to stand, Arabella promptly decided to hide under the bed rather than in it. She lay down flat on her stomach against the floor, and began to worm her way underneath the bed.

Ice-cold fingers grabbed her ankle. Arabella opened her mouth to let out a piercing scream——and a tremendously loud sneeze came out instead. It flew out with such force that her head smacked up into the bed slats.

"Ow," whispered Arabella.

Her ankle was released.

There was a thud, as of a shoe thrown against a wall, and a petulant sob.

"Oh," wailed a spectral voice, in a surprisingly un-spectral manner, "this *beastly* entrance exam! And only fifteen minutes left in the Eve — there goes my chance at Spooks' Select Academy for another year."

The apparition sounded much like any of the girls back at boarding school in Hampstead — probably freckled, and scrawny, and prone to catarrh. Its tone of lamentation was all too familiar to Miss Aberdeen, whose eyes had oft despairing wept over an end-of-term paper. Arabella's bottom wriggled backwards, out from below the bed. Cautiously, the rest of her emerged.

"Yes," she whispered, her voice scarcely more than a bark in her throat. "Exams are... horrid things."

"Aren't they *just*," her visitor agreed bitterly, and stuck two transparent feet out of the wainscoting.

Arabella sat up. It was an immense relief to find that the ghost did not harbour malicious intentions after all.

The ghost emerged fully from the wall and stood in front of Arabella. She looked a scrawny young figure, tall and bony at the joints, with a great mass of long, curling hair. A scarf was tied around her head, beneath her hair, hiding her eye sockets. She was almost completely transparent, and her spectral form reflected strange glints of rainbow colour when she moved, like a soap bubble. Above her hovered a pair of eyes, complete with pale eyelids and luxuriously thick lashes. "My name's Esther Blewett, by the by."

"Arabella," whispered the young lady of that name.

The faint outline of a paper floated out of the wainscot and drifted through the air. The ghost reached out with her thin hands and grabbed it. Her fingernails were grubby and showed signs of a great deal of nervous chewing. The eyes winked out of sight and materialised a moment later near her shoulder, goggling down at the paper.

"I always get through Section One tolerably, you know — 'prompt your Subject to summon a servant; use of room temperature and mild noises permitted'. I thought the phonograph in Section Two was rather clever of me, unlike a *certain Millicent Maynard,* whose papa hired a full phantasmal chorus from Oxford. But 'pride goeth before destruction', so Section Three was unsurprisingly a disaster. Section Four permits phenomena, which should've gone off all right, except that I muffed it with the broken glass. That wasn't supposed to happen. I only wanted to wiggle it some, for effect..." She sniffled, growing more tearful. "And now I've talked to you, which disqualifies me from Sections Five and Six, which are to be conducted without—" (the ghost consulted the paper in her hand) "—'screams, wails, unearthly moans, keening, or vocal utterances of any kind' ... oh, misery, misery!"

"But you spoke to me earlier," whispered Arabella, tugging a blanket round her shoulders.

"Pooh! Of course I did!" said Esther, wiping invisible tears from her nose with the back of her hand. "Each portion of the test has different requirements — didn't you hear me explaining?"

She mashed the paper into a ball and flung it at the ceiling, where it vanished. The eyes bobbing at her shoulder likewise disappeared.

"Well, I concede defeat. Fifty Christmas Eves I've been trying, and you're the most vexatious subject I've struck yet. Even the old gentleman last year was decent enough to grant me a few croaks as he ran out of the room." The ghost gave a wistful sigh. "But the panellists said he didn't sound scared enough. They're awf'lly strict, you know."

Arabella felt rather helpless, and then, rather guilty. These emotions were rapidly succeeded by a strange melting warmth — a certain kindling of goodwill towards men, and towards sad, distressed ghosts, too. It was Christmas Eve, after all.

"Well," she said, hoarsely, "perhaps I can cry a bit. Or attempt a few wails."

"Oh, would you?" The ghost's eyes, tearful and translucent, appeared on the floorboards at Arabella's feet.

Arabella stiffened, the blood thrilling in her veins. It cost her some effort to speak again, with those eyes bulging up at her. She shivered. "P-possibly."

"I'd be ever so obliged."

Arabella took a deep breath and summoned all the lung power at her command. The noise that came out in response was pitiful — like a squeak of air escaping a rubber balloon. She looked alarmed, and prodded feebly at her swollen throat.

"Do keep trying," urged the spectre, in agonised tones.

Arabella obliged. The ghost's eyes fixed themselves anxiously above the clock face, while the body crossed its arms and looked equal parts hopeful and gloomy.

At last, Arabella managed to coax a scream out of her throat, and just as the shriek rang out, so too did the Midnight bells, declaring it Christmas Day. The ghost gave her a delighted smile that stretched as wide as the room, before she vanished with the last peal of the church bells.

Several moments later, the footman came hastening down the passage. The door opened, just a crack, and an enquiring eyebrow appeared.

"All right in there, miss? I heard a scream."

Arabella paused. Mr. Morris was not a man to whom one could easily explain that Oxenhoath's second-best guest room had recently been used as a kind of examination hall for the afterlife.

"Sorry," said Arabella, meekly. "A beetle ran over my foot."

The End

the haunted specter

E.B. GRIMM

IT WAS NOT customary in her country to travel after a death in the family, but then again, it was not customary in her country to be forcibly driven away from one's household either. So Enid Breckford's situation could hardly be considered customary by anyone.

But at last, when the eastern school she taught at shut down for lack of funding, and the widow that hosted her passed away, for the first time in years she did what was expected of her, and she went home for Christmas.

When her feet touched down in her own town, it was Christmas Eve, three years less a day since she last left her own city, with its cobblestones and chill fog and evergreens and cloaked street goers. It was all so familiar and yet so strange, after all her time spent among the jewels, the spices, the shimmering hot nights and the perpetually wet-leafed trees of her eastern sojourn. Enid and her luggage wandered slowly through the streets, observing the street lamps being lit, the sound of caroling in the air, and the merry greetings exchanged between friends and strangers. It felt good to hug a woolen coat tightly round herself again; even though it was an unseasonably warm Christmas for her country, it had been three years less a day since she'd needed a coat at all. So she fingered the scarlet wool with a faint smile, taking pleasure in its familiar scratchiness after all this time.

The streets got more and more desolate the closer she drew to her destination—or perhaps it was only her mindset that became more desolate, but it seemed there were fewer mirthful voices around, less greenery on the doors, and almost no good smells wafting through the air. So it felt no coincidence that by the time the town clock struck six, and she rounded the corner to her sprawling family home, not a single sign of Christmas cheer remained, and her only accompaniment in the foggy December twilight was a flickering light in the window of the mansion's east garret.

Enid squinted thoughtfully at the window, brushing an escaped curl out of her face. It would have been odd for her father to be in the east garret, up that precarious staircase...so it was likely one of the servants.

She rounded the porch, walked up the great front steps, and rang the doorbell after a moment's hesitation, her hand shaking ever so slightly in its gray glove.

It seemed an eternity 'til it was answered, but all of a sudden the door came open, and the man within said, in a hoarse voice, "So you're back, are you?"

Enid looked the man up and down. His dressing gown was the same as always, except far more threadbare, and he was frighteningly thin, his blue eyes burning like angry fire in his lined face. He had not shaved, and an untidy beard was coming in.

What was most surprising, however, was that he was answering the door in the first place. Certainly Lord Meriweather Breckford could afford a butler.

She extended a cautious hand. "Happy Christmas, Father."

Her father raised an eyebrow, and then, without taking her hand, said, flatly, "Come in and have tea."

• • •

Tea was not all she remembered it to be in the Breckford household. To begin with, Father insisted she take her coat and gloves off, but she found it was freezing in the house—no fire lit anywhere, just one sputtering oil lamp on the tea table itself. The tea was boiled to the point of bitterness, and the biscuits tasted as though the butter in them had soured. The eggs, at least, were good, and she ate four, whilst Father watched her from his great armchair, a cup of harsh-smelling tea in his wrinkled hand, his hollow cheeks looking ghastly in the dim light.

Finally Enid said, carefully, for the sake of breaking the silence, "I think perhaps we ought to get the servants to bring up some different food, Father—there seems to be something a little odd about a lot of this."

"My board not good enough for you?" inquired her father, and as he spoke he leaned down and fished a bottle and a little silver case from underneath the table.

"No, I just think perhaps you—might not be noticing the way the tea tastes," faltered Enid, as she watched her father pour a liberal amount of bourbon into his half-empty cup.

He responded with nothing but a grunt, drained the cup, then poured himself another, remarking abruptly, "Didn't expect you back."

Enid swallowed, watching him light a cigar from his case. "Didn't...didn't really expect to be back. How have things been?"

"Same as ever. Impossible to get help, and what you can get is worthless. Don't get many callers, but that's the way I like it."

"Do you get out much?"

His icy eyes glinted at her; he said nothing.

"Well," she said, trying to keep her teeth from chattering, "I've enjoyed my time abroad. I know you said 'take a holiday at Breckford expense', but I've paid my own way aside from ship fares, working as a schoolteacher, so I've brought back most of the money."

"Keep it. You'll need it to go back again."

Enid took another bitter swallow of tea. "I assume that means you'd rather I not stay."

Her father's lip curled slightly, but his voice was expressionless as he answered. "Not unless you've changed a good deal."

Enid traced the pattern of the carpet with her boot tip, trying not to cough on cigar smoke.

"I'm uncertain how it is you wanted me to change, Father."

Lord Breckford regarded her in unblinking silence. A minute passed, and Enid said, with a faint note of desperation, "I brought back some curiosities from the foreign lands for you, as a Christmas gift—"

"Don't want your things."

"Oh. Well, what would you like then? Everybody must have some gift on Christmas." She forced a smile.

Another long, gruff silence. Then, so sharply it made her jump, "You could get rid of the ghost in the garret for me."

At first she wasn't sure he was serious—he'd played some awful jokes in the past. But his set scowl proved the truth.

"There's a ghost in the garret?" she tried to sound as if this conversation, too, was natural.

"Yes. Blasted specter won't let me alone these past years. Makes it hard to get servants—they've spread 'round to each other that the place is haunted."

"Ah," said poor Enid, struggling valiantly to maintain a neutral expression.

"I'd be very grateful to be rid of it," and those awful eyes glittered at her.

"Well—I mean, I'm not quite sure I'm knowledgeable about how to get rid of a ghost, Father—"

"Smart enough to be a schoolteacher," and he took another swig of his 'tea.'

He clearly wasn't changing his mind; she leaned forward and said, firmly, "If you're sure that's what you want."

He regarded her in silence.

"All right then. I'll go up and have a go right now—that way we can have a happy Christmas," and she nearly choked on her last words.

"Take the lamp," said he. "I don't mind the dark."

So she took the lamp, and headed out into the vast emptiness of the hall, trying to make her footsteps even and measured.

As soon as she got out of the sitting room, she took a great, gasping breath of the stale, freezing air and stood for a moment trying to get her bearings.

Ghost in the garret...he had really cracked the rest of the way, hadn't he?

"Well, nothing for it," she murmured, and headed for the stairs. It was probably that some animal had become trapped up there, and while she didn't particularly fancy chasing a bat out of the attic by herself, if it earned her father's good graces, it was worth it.

She soon found herself climbing the rickety, spiraling attic staircase at the end of the vast, echoing back hallway. Enid had always detested how unsteady the staircase was, but in recent years it had become nearly untraversable—the railing looked like a breath of wind could blow it away, and the steps groaned as she placed her boot tips on them.

"What a hazard," she muttered, trying not to think of the floor far below her, trying not to think about the bat at the top of the stairs, trying not to think of the old man with those same old rings on his fingers in the sitting room.

The latch of the trapdoor at the top was worn almost through, contrary to her memory. She flipped the door open and placed the lamp on the floor beyond, then hoisted herself into the room.

Once her boots were on solid floorboards again, she retrieved her lamp, brushed off her skirt, and took stock of her surroundings.

The garret of their manor was vast in both length and width, one giant room that was deathly quiet and ought to have been pitch dark.

But at the far west end, for some reason, there was a lamp burning, and as Enid squinted in confusion at the light, a dark humanoid silhouette moved in front of the light—

The lamp went out.

Enid clapped a hand over her mouth to keep herself from screaming. Any thoughts of 'bats' vanished from her mind. She practically scrambled back out of the trapdoor and onto the staircase.

Echoing footsteps sounded from the hallways where she'd come, and she heard her father's voice, cackling to himself as he moved in her direction.

For a moment she stood there, trembling, trapped between the terrifying unknown of the room above and the terrifying known of the rooms beyond.

Then she turned back to the garret.

The light had remained off, and she clutched her own lamp a little tighter; feeble as its flicker was, in this vast space, it was better than nothing.

Enid stood for a moment, holding her breath, listening.

Something was in the darkness with her. She could sense its presence even if she couldn't hear it moving.

"Hello." She steadied her shaking voice, "I'm the daughter in this household, and I've come to ask you to leave."

Silence.

Silence so complete it thrummed in her ears.

Enid swallowed, hard, and began to take cautious shuffling steps towards the window where the lamp had been placed. She had a sudden flash of recollection from her walk in earlier—whoever, whatever was in here had been up here as she was approaching the manor.

Not a ghost though, surely it was just some sort of...

Her brain grappled for a natural explanation, and as it did she brushed up against something in the darkness, something inexplicably cold and silky to the touch.

Enid smothered a scream, jumped back, and then reached out to the same spot again, hurriedly trying to verify it was just a curtain that the flickering shadows of her lamp weren't picking up.

Not only was there nothing there, but her light went out—and she heard a swift exhale, as though someone had blown it.

Her own breathing sounded hoarse and ragged in the darkness, faster and faster, as she stood rooted to the floor, terrified to move, terrified *not* to move.

Slowly her eyes began to adjust to the little bit of moonlight streaming in through the window— she certainly couldn't head back for the trapdoor with no light—she'd fall and break her neck if she tried to climb the stairs like that. Perhaps there were some matches by the other lamp... or perhaps whatever it was would take mercy on her.

Enid opened her mouth to speak again, but couldn't make her voice work; she took another step and the floorboard creaked, not under her foot but across the empty room, behind her. A few more steps, and she struggled to remain calm, as the garret boards whined eerily from every direction but under her own feet.

To her left she noticed the vague outline of a table and chairs, which surprised her, as this part of the garret had historically been empty. A strange form seemed to be sitting at the head of the table.

She froze again, trying to discern if the figure in the chair was responding to her movement at all. It seemed not to, so she came a little closer and put out a trembling hand to pat it on the shoulder.

It slumped over like a dead thing at her faint touch, so she could only assume, in this light, that it was a dummy, or a strangely placed jacket.

Or a dead thing.

She withdrew her hand quickly, but the grain of that wool under her fingers had felt freakishly familiar. A glance at the table itself showed a grouping of what appeared to be picture frames, and something golden that caught the moonlight. She couldn't make out anything else but she cautiously picked up one of the frames to look at when she reached the window.

Another groan from across the room, and a barely-audible whisper...

Good riddance.

For some reason it was that sound that made Enid snap; she shrieked and charged for the window, her panic growing as she realized her feet still made no sound but the walls on either side were shaking slightly.

She reached the windowsill where the other lamp had been placed and scrabbled around for matches—nothing. Not even the lamp itself.

The timbers around her began to settle, but the silence was almost worse and she pressed her back to the wall, the moonlight coming past her to illuminate the room beyond.

"Who's there?" her voice shook wretchedly.

More silence. She realized the picture frame was still in her hand. Cautiously, she turned it over to have a look.

It was a photograph of a young man in a wool coat, a young man with dark hair and laughing eyes, and sickness lines in his face.

And she, Enid, was standing next to the man in the photo, with her blond curls and her long skirts, hugging him and grinning.

She exhaled sharply.

It all made sense. The familiar coat, the familiar voice.

She straightened and said flatly, "Edward, is that you?"

Silence.

Enid's lip trembled, but she wasn't scared anymore.

"I'm not going to hurt you or anything, you know..."

Silence, then out of the darkness, a hoarse voice said, "Nobody can do that any more than they have."

Enid swallowed. "Come where I can see you."

A bitter laugh, and then a faint, blueish shape stepped into the moonlight.

It was Edward all right, in his shirtsleeves and waistcoat,

painfully gaunt as she had last seen him. The resentment in his transparent eyes was new.

The picture frame slipped from Enid's hands, and the glass shattered on the floor. She said, her voice cracking, "Why are you here?"

The ghost of her brother regarded her coldly, and without a response. The room's silence thrummed in Enid's ears again, and she found herself pressing against the wall ever so slightly. There was familiarity in the shape across from her, true, but there was also something eerily alien about it.

She tried again to gain a response. "Father said there was a ghost, but he didn't say it was you."

The silence grew more oppressive. The ghost had not moved once, and Enid began to think her mind was playing tricks on her— she advanced slowly, and reached out a hand, whilst the pale, motionless figure's eyes followed her movements.

Her hand brushed his chest and he recoiled swiftly. There was a sharp crack of the boards across the room, and she instinctively shook her hand to rid it of the silky coldness that was now her brother.

Edward moved closer to her again, and stood there with his hands in his pockets, his eyes now avoiding her. The haggardness of his face became more apparent now she was closer to him—not even in his last illness had he looked this weary. Every line of his spectral frame spoke of exhaustion.

Enid folded her arms, tapping her boot on the floor thoughtfully. Then she said, low, "You look tired, Ed. Like you'd kill for a little rest."

Edward still wouldn't look at her, but he gave a quick, terse nod.

Enid scratched her head thoughtfully. "So it's not your choice to be here?"

He shook his head.

Something about him looked a little more like himself just then, and Enid asked, her lip trembling a bit, "What's it about then? What can I do for you, dear?"

Edward looked stricken for a moment. There was a cold rush of air so violent that some of Enid's hair came loose from its knot.

She set her jaw and approached him again.

"Come on, Ed. Talk to me. Tell me how I can help you."

He opened his mouth, and his face convulsed, as though he was struggling with himself, then he said, in a barely audible croak, "Can't...speak much."

"I know," said Enid softly. "Show me, if you can."

His face twisted again, then he stretched out his right hand to her, not as though he wished her to take it, but as if there was something to see about it.

Enid stared at it, a sinking feeling in her stomach at the thought that the strange, ghostly appendage belonged to what was left of her brother.

Something didn't seem right aside from its transparency, though. She cocked her head to one side.

"There's...there's something missing. Where's that ring you always wore that I gave you?"

Edward's face crumpled, but this time he did not speak. Instead, a single dark tear slid down his insubstantial face.

Enid looked away for fear she would cry herself—then noticed, again, something golden on the long table catching the moonlight.

"Ed—it's over there, isn't it?"

Without waiting for a confirmation, she rushed over to the table and her fingers found the gold. It was indeed the familiar shape of the ring she had given her little brother on his eighteenth birthday. By her recollection, he'd been buried with it, so she had no idea why it would be here.

Unless...

Edward had drifted over to stand behind her and she said, gritting her teeth, "Did Father take this from you?"

Edward nodded, his eyebrows drawn together angrily, and a cold blast of air went through the room again.

Enid turned it over in her hands, considering.

"And you can't rest without it, it would seem. Does he know that? Does he know how tired you are?"

Edward's face was strained again, and the frame of the entire garret seemed to strain with him, by the sound of it. The floor shook, and Enid clutched the edge of the table for support.

Then the whole place hushed all at once, and in the silence, her brother's voice came, ragged and furious.

"Yes."

Without hesitating, Enid put the ring in her pocket, and tucked the coat from the table over her arm. The exhausted face across from her was both inquisitive and terrified.

"I'm going to put it back for you," she said, her heart beating faster as she thought of what that might mean.

Edward struggled again, then managed the words, "He'll hurt you."

And with that statement, for the first time, Enid fully saw her brother in both the form and tone of the specter.

But she shrugged, and started for the stairs, calling gently over her shoulder.

"Nobody can do that any more than they have."

She paused, waiting for a response, but there was instead a heavy silence, broken only by the sound of the attic timbers settling around her.

Then the trapdoor slammed open and she started with a little shriek.

A tottering shape emerged like a nightmare from the staircase and Enid was reminded again of how much taller and broader her father was than her, even now when he was ailing. He looked at her with eyes full of hatred, his lamp illuminating every crag and cranny in his aged face, and he was more terrifying than any ghost ever could have been.

Enid clutched the coat in one hand for comfort, the ring heavy in her pocket. She said, in a level tone, "I'm going out to the graveyard, Father."

Her father glanced over her shoulder, and spat on the ground.

"I see you've found this whining brother of yours, then."

The room became colder all of a sudden, and Enid bit her lip.

"He's not whining. He's just tired, Father. I want him to be able to rest."

Her words were brave but her knees were shaking, and she knew all too well what would soon follow.

"Rest," snarled her father, kicking unsteadily at the floor. "Rest! He can rot in his grave or in my garret; all that matters is that I love him, and if that's not enough for him he's a wretch."

"He's not," said Enid, desperately. Sour nausea rose in her throat, and she was tempted to cover her own ears.

The lamp her father held caught the flash of madness in his eyes as he ranted heedlessly on, his voice raising with every word. "You, my girl, are even worse. At least he died before he could give me any grief in his life. Meanwhile you don't even have the courtesy to leave me alone and rid me of the burden of you."

Enid knew his rage all too well, and old memories of pain were resurfacing like a hurricane in her head.

But this time, to her surprise, some of her own rage surfaced as well; the thought of the exhausted shape of her brother behind her... and the three years less a day she'd been an exile, on the whim of a heavy-fisted old man.

The same man was advancing on her now, his hand raised to strike her, as of years past. Something in Enid snapped. She straightened up and clutched the coat tighter.

As his hobbling form loomed over her, poised to lay the blow, she said quietly, firmly, "Enough."

And as if they had planned it, the floor shook wildly, and behind her a voice more her brother's than ever shouted, "*Enough!*"

With that the light went out, and her father roared wordlessly at Edward.

She heard the old man's halting feet stumbling around, and backwards as he searched for her in the darkness.

"Ed, the trapdoor!" she cried urgently, rushing out with both arms outstretched to try and prevent disaster.

A bloodcurdling scream, and the sound of cracking wood. Enid was at the edge of the hole and looked down just in time to see her father's limp body, having broken through the rickety stair railing, hit the floor several stories below.

She heard herself shriek but felt as numb as if she'd been plunged into cold water. She clambered through the hole and down the stairs, so fast she was in danger of falling herself.

Edward's voice rang out, strained and sorrowful above her.

"He's dead."

Enid reached the bottom and looked down at his unmoving body. She extended a hand, then withdrew it, whispering, "How do you know?"

But there came no answer.

The venerable streets of the old town that had seen Enid walk through with her luggage only an hour earlier now saw her barreling along without a coat or hat towards the police station.

When she told the story to the police chief, he said, with a kindness she almost resented, "Don't take it too hard, Miss Breckford. We've had so many reports, and have been expecting some accident or disaster with your father for years now."

"I shouldn't have left him," she murmured, and the police chief shook his head.

"I'm not sure anybody could've got through to him, Miss. Believe me, we tried."

Enid felt cold and empty, and she clutched her brother's coat tighter to her as she left the station, realizing for the first time it was still in her hands.

The streets were quieter now than when she had come in. Everyone was having family tea, and she passed many lighted windows with little portraits of families within them, eating Christmas Eve dinner. Enid had almost forgot it was Christmas but it was good to see the merriment now, after the horror of the past hour.

Eventually she reached the old graveyard, and made for her mother's grave, in that same old corner tucked away beside the cedar grove.

There was a grave she didn't recognize next to it. She leaned over and inspected the inscription.

Edward Breckford, 20 years old. Loved by his family, dearly missed.

"A little too dearly in one case," she murmured, and strode across to the pine trees in search of a gob of sap. She returned with one and stuck the ring to the bottom of the empty stone vase, then tore down some brightly colored holly branches from another nearby bush and filled the vase with them atop of the ring.

She straightened from her work and dusted off her hands, then shivered, looking around. The town clock was striking, and it was pitch black around now but for the moonlight. Edward's coat was lying in a little pile by his grave, so Enid fetched it and shrugged it on.

It had been a long time since she'd worn her brother's coat, and she stood over his grave now, her hands limply in its pockets.

"I hope that did it, Ed," she whispered.

She thought, for a moment, she saw a faint, ghostly form in the act of lying down atop the grave plot...and then there was a long sigh.

Perhaps it was the wind, but something in the air spoke of peace and she heaved a sigh herself, then looked around again.

It was Christmas Eve, and she was in a graveyard.

Yet somehow she belonged and was happy here far more than she had been in that freezing parlor, where the old man had glowered at her, and she had not been allowed to put on her coat.

Here she was warm at least.

A single tear streaked down Enid's face, and she said, softly, as the wind blew the long grasses around her skirts. "I'm sorry. I'm so sorry. What he did to you was not your fault."

It could've been her imagination, but she thought she heard that fretful wind carry back to her, in her brother's voice, similar words.

I'm so sorry. What he did to you was not your fault.

Enid stared dully for a moment, then managed a faint smile through her tears. "Thank you, Edward."

She didn't particularly fancy going home, so she went to sit with her back to the old pine tree, her brother's coat still warm around her, while the chill wind blew through her curls, and the town lights beyond the graveyard twinkled with merriment.

And after a little while, she remarked to the thin air, laughing slightly, "Well, Ed, I'm finally doing what's customary and expected of me. Spending Christmas with my family."

Enid was awoken the next morning, for the first time in three years, by the sound of her own city's church bells hearkening to early Christmas Mass. And when she hastened out of the graveyard in search of the church, she took the coat with her, with a murmur of 'happy Christmas' to her brother's grave, and a strange conviction in her heart that perhaps she was not so alone as it seemed.

For "Ed." Thank you.

the pale horse

GRACE F. HOPKINS

IT WAS Christmas Eve and in the fading grey twilight, everything sparkled. From the ice on the pine boughs to the hoarfrost on the sparse scrub brush, to the eaves and shingles of the cottage at Rhys' back. Smoke plumed from the chimneys of all the houses at his back, each lit within by firelight, and overflowing with music and laughter. It all felt suffocating to him.

So he escaped into the open land behind the house, to the solitary world wrapped in stillness. He had a horse skull to find, and even though he could have searched for it any other day, it was an excuse. An excuse to be alone with nothing but the land, the sky, and his grief.

His cheeks were still warm with wassail and the glow of firelight, but the tip of his nose was cold. His hands were plunged into the depths of his pockets. He hadn't paused to grab mittens, or to tell anyone where he was going. He'd simply left the moment he'd been beyond anyone's gaze and let the door clatter closed behind him, praying the boisterous talk of his family was enough to drown the sound.

It would be Mari Lwyd soon and it'd been Jac who'd asked him if they'd gotten the head for their pale horse yet. In truth, Mari Lwyd had been the last thing on Rhys' mind, though he normally anticipated it each year. It felt almost wanton, garish now, to don silly costumes and traipse through town in a drunken giddiness, knocking on neighbors' doors for carols and riddles and jokes. But even if he didn't want to attend this year, he knew the other lads would, and they all knew Rhys' old brood mare had finally given up the ghost a few months ago. They'd let her turn to carrion, and he still knew where she lay.

His Mam would likely see through his excuse, whether he returned triumphant with the skull or not. It was a strange thing to do, abandoning house on Christmas Eve, when all those that Rhys loved were underneath one roof for the first time in months.

Well, almost all.

All of the talk and the song and the chatter and cheer couldn't fill the empty chair in the corner of the room. Nor hide the subtle sorrow that clung to everything. It couldn't now erase the tears that'd coated his mother's lashes this morning, as she'd pressed her nose to a disused stocking they no longer hung at the fireplace. It couldn't staunch the desperate guilt that clawed at Rhys' throat like some wild beast.

So here he was, learning to breathe again in the press of the setting sun, begging the chilled air to shock some sense back into him. He walked a quarter of a mile toward the back pasture wall without quite knowing it. His boots were wearing thin at the toes, and his stockings needed mending, so now the cold crept in and tingles raced over his aching feet each time he took a step. But no matter. No matter. No matter. It was honestly a blessing to feel anything.

He paused at the stone stacked pasture wall and sighed, the swirl of his breath spiraling toward the faint stars just starting to eche an existence out of the murky sky. All the sheep were in for the night, and without the sparse pointillism of their white bodies, the landscape lay barren and foreign.

He made a right and began his quest again, head down, looking through the scrub brush for a horse's skull, praying he didn't overlook it in the gathering dark.

Harri and Gwen had hugged him warmly upon their arrival this afternoon, and it had caught Rhys a bit by surprise. None of them blamed him, he'd been told. At the funeral they had all hugged him just the same as any, had squeezed him just as tightly, had held him just as dearly. Now was no different.

But that didn't change the fact that last time they'd all been under one roof together was that funeral in the spring. A funeral caused by Rhys' own negligence. Their forgiveness and solidarity, so undeserving, won so easily, didn't change the fact that were it not for Rhys, his Mam and Tad wouldn't have had to bury one of their children last March. Were it not for Rhys, there wouldn't be an empty bed in the loft, and an empty place at the table.

It had felt like a cruel tableau this morning, helping Mam prepare for Christmas. He'd gone through the motions as usual, dragging spare pallets from the barn for their guests, simmering the wassail, baking the nut bread and sweeping the hay loft clean. All of their actions spoke 'Christmas,' but Rhys' heart hadn't been in it. Neither, it seemed, had Mam's. She did everything mechanically, a far-off look in her eyes. And he'd worked beside her, mutely, a marionette on tangled strings.

Despite the fact that the younger ones had their fill of nightmares in the days just after, Rhys was still impressed by their resilience. He knew they missed Nia with a ferocity that showed itself in early days with fits of passion and nights spent crying in the wee hours. But now, their young minds found a way to fixate only on the magic of Christmas, instead of focusing on what they'd lost. He envied them.

Somewhere in the pines beyond the pasture wall, an owl hooted, its call cutting through the night like a scythe through hay. Despite himself, Rhys jumped. He'd almost begun to believe, with the cottages left behind, that he was the only living thing here in the gathering dark.

It was nights like these when he was by himself in the stillness that he could almost believe all of the old tales that haunted these lands, about the mysterious and roaming Wild Hunt. Or the giants and brownies that slumbered just out of sight. Or the wails of the *Cyhyraeth* and the howls of *Cwn Annwn* that would portend one's death.

If Nia had heard the wails of the *Cyhyraeth* or the baying of the *Cwn Annwn* before her death— well, Rhys would never know. She was dead by the time he found her, lying wide-eyed behind the old spinning shed.

Rhys was certain of very few things, but he knew with a visceral conviction that he'd never forget her face that day. Though her chest was still and her face disfigured by the swelling, he wrenched her mouth open, pressed his mouth to hers and tried to inflate her lungs with his own breath. He'd tried to breathe life back into his sister's corpse as the other children around him had sobbed and screamed. Until his own sobs had risen from within and aborted his desperate hope. It was those screams and those cries that rang in his ears most nights, more than an imagined symphony of hunting horns or any mournful howls of mythic dogs.

Rhys stumbled on the rutted ground, and he side-stepped quickly to correct his momentum. He paused and breathed in deeply, shaking off the memory. He wasn't out here just to take a stroll. He had to focus. He had a horse skull to find. He may be out here to escape his grief, but if he dressed up his time away with the trappings of festivity, perhaps he could avoid a lecture from his Mam or questions about how he was faring.

Besides, if he couldn't find this horse skull, he'd have to ask one of the other lads in town for one. For years it had been Rhys who'd been the voice of their pale horse, hiding beneath the white sheet and the broomstick with the horse skull fastened on the end. But the last thing he felt like doing was going house-to-house telling jokes and riddles and trying to charm the neighbors into letting him and his accompanying pack of masked tricksters in for a drink. The last thing he really wanted was to organize this when that would actually require *talking* to people, something he hadn't quite done in months. He didn't really want to start now.

He knew he must look like a hermit. He could see that accusation on Harri's face clear enough when he'd ushered him and Gwen into the house this afternoon.

"You alrigh'?" Harri had asked, stepping over the threshold and shaking some mist off his hat. But it hadn't been merely a customary greeting, there had been a real question in his words. His eyes had raked him over, a frown forming between his brows.

Though Jac had grown taller since the funeral this spring, his ankles showing out the bottom of his trousers—Rhys hadn't quite noticed until yesterday morning, when Jac had been the one to hang the garland on the parlor eves. Sara too had begun to fill out, turning from a knobby child into a proper girl with curves and soft edges. And when Gwen had followed Harri into the house today, her belly round with a growing babe— it seemed everyone else had blossomed since this spring. All except for Rhys. Instead he notched his belt a few holes tighter these days, and grew his beard thick to hide his thinning cheeks.

Something white caught his eye against the brownness of rutted earth, and a flash of satisfaction rose. Not three yards ahead, littered across the ground were bones.

The ribcage jutted skyward, curled tips brown and caked with dirt. The spine was mostly intact. Rhys picked up his pace and nearly tripped over a lone hoof lying in his path. He counted femurs and scapula and vertebrae, but found no skull in the detritus.

He spun in a circle, but still, no skull leered up at him. He paced further, but while all the other bones remained fairly well accounted for— the skull was conspicuously missing.

Of course. It was just his luck. Perhaps if he'd come out here even a couple weeks ago he might have found it and rescued it from scavengers.

But he hadn't been quick enough. He was never quick enough.

He hadn't been quick enough that day in early spring either—and of all the things he blamed himself for— that one was foremost.

In the days after, a litany of accusations had pressed down on his shoulders— more suffocating than six feet of dirt. He ought to have checked the shed for bee hives. He ought to have suggested they only play in front of the house. He ought to have insisted Sara or Jac hide *with* Nia. He ought not to have acquiesced to Nia's plea of 'just one more game.'

He ought to have sought her first. Found her faster. Maybe then there'd still have been a soul in her body, breath in her lungs when he'd finally found her. And perhaps she could have made it. He could have— she could have—

A cry of frustration bubbled up and Rhys groaned aloud, kicking the frozen ground. His cry echoed off the stolid trees, hazy behind his cloud of breath. He stuffed his hands back inside his pockets. His fingers were red and numb now, and his legs ached with cold. He'd best go back home, before Harri or Tad decided to come looking for him.

He stood for several seconds, under the light of the rising moon — swollen and yellow and low at the horizon— big enough to cast his shadow behind him, but his feet could not be coaxed toward home.

He wanted to melt into the trees and disappear. He wanted to lay down with the bones around his feet and decompose too. He wanted to disappear to some other reality, to some other world where Nia wasn't dead and it wasn't his fault and it wasn't his first Christmas without her.

He wanted—A flash of white flitted among the trees to his right. For a moment he assumed it was a bird. But it came again and with it, the sound of hoof-beats.

Rhys turned and squinted into trees beyond the stone stacked wall of his pasture, and there, nose snuffling the ground among the pines was an impossibly beautiful and impossibly tall white mare.

For a moment his mouth ran dry. He blinked, scrubbed at his

eyes. But the mare remained, rump now turned toward him, walking through the underbrush with no sound of cracking twigs, only the sound of rhythmic hoofbeats.

Were it not Christmas Eve and were his mind not on the old tales, he might have assumed one his neighbors' mares had jumped a fence. But as the mare wandered deeper into the wood, he noticed with no small amount of astonishment that she was *glowing,* shifting like a shaft of self-made moonlight. A shiver of fear ran through him. Either he was out of his mind, or he was seeing something few mortal eyes had ever been privy to see.

But there was no time to speculate, the mare was walking away, and so abandoning his quest for a dead mare's skull, he jogged to the pasture wall, vaulted it— and followed the ghostly horse into the depths of the forest.

He hadn't seen this mare around town, that was for certain. It was beautiful: immaculately clean, perfectly groomed, and built more finely than a horse for a king, not at all like the squat and hay-bellied horses in this village. It scarcely made a sound as it swept its way through the forest.

A feeling of dream swept over Rhys as he followed it between the trees. A surreal calm filled him and his mind—so prone to questions and commentaries— was all but silent. Instinctually he knew he was meant to be following this mare, following because she was *leading* him somewhere.

She was outpacing him, but only just, each step around a tree trunk or each skirt around a bush rewarded him with the sight of her white rump, the flick of her pale tail. The trees grew close in here, thick. They were wandering into the part of the forest that was untamed, the undergrowth, even in winter, groping upward.

He followed the mare for a mile, maybe more, but no matter how he tried to jog to catch her, or no matter how his progress was thwarted by the brambles or felled limbs, she was always equidistant from him. So close, and yet just out of reach.

But as Rhys passed into a clearing, suddenly, he lost her. He stood in a circle of old yews, and though he swore he'd also seen the mare enter here, there was no sign of her now. There was no way of knowing which way she'd passed through the clearing and where she now led.

A panicky frustration welled in him. He'd followed a phantom into the wood, and now he was miles from home with no clear way of finding his way back. The boughs of the evergreens still stretched thick and many above him. It was darkening rapidly now, and the moonlight and stars were but faint scratches above.

He would be stranded out here before long, alone without a light but for the small matchbox in his pocket. He had wanted a moment alone, yes. But if he was out too long, they'd start to worry. And he didn't fancy spending all night out in the cold. If he were truly lost, how long would it take him to get back? All night? Would he even miss midnight Mass?

He stepped further into the clearing and tried to regain his bearings, neck craned upward to locate the moon. She could guide him if he found her. As he stepped further into the clearing, a shiver raced through his body and the hair on his arms stood on end. It was as if a bucket of cold water had been splashed upon him. The air left his lungs.

A voice spoke behind him from amidst the trees, clear as a bell, "Come find me!"

He turned. A flash of white. Then nothing.

He didn't hesitate. He barreled in the direction of that voice. For he knew that voice, and the flash of blonde hair, silvery in the moonlight.

"Nia!" he called. His voice shattered the quiet of the forest like a gunshot through a briar glen.

That was the last thing she'd ever spoken to him as he'd stood in the kitchen and performatively covered his eyes, beginning to count down from fifty.

"Come find me."

But where was she leading? Where was she hiding now? His footsteps thundered through the underbrush as he ran blindly, searching desperately.

Laughter sounded to the left of him, as if she were enjoying his bewilderment. "Over here!"

He turned to see her small frame, slipping between two trees like water among rock.

He followed. "Nia, wait!"

"Come find me!" she called. But she did not wait.

Much like the horse before, he was always behind, never within reach. His lungs burned and his legs ached, but unlike how she'd been in life, Nia was faster.

Was this a dream? Or some sick punishment? Was this his destiny, to always chase but never catch?

Tears formed in his eyes, but they were not from the wind. An ache seized his chest, but it was not from the exertion. "Nia, wait!" he gasped. And it was a plea. A prayer.

But she did not wait and soon he was bursting from the tree-line on the other side of the forest and standing in an open and sparse field, blanketed in hoarfrost.

His stomach sank and fear squeezed his throat as he realized just *exactly* where he was. Rising out of the landscape, like the spine of some sleeping beast were the barrows, spaced apart at somewhat regular intervals, foreboding and solemn in the moonlight. These were not mere relics of a bygone age, though. No. Rhys was all too familiar with *these* barrows in particular.

Nia had died just after St. Dydd's Day, when the ground was still frozen and far too hard for spades to cut a full six feet deep. They had to wait for the thaw to come in earnest before they could bury her proper, in the cemetery by St. Asaph. So they'd kept her casket in a barrow until then. One of *these* barrows.

And grazing at the far side of the barrows, as if having waited for him, was the pale mare.

"Why did you bring me here?" Rhys whispered. He wasn't sure if he expected the mare to answer, but he felt the need to voice the question.

Images flashed through his mind of the day they'd laid Nia in the ground, sliding her small casket beneath the mound of raised earth like they were sacrificing her to the maw of some hungry monster. The first daffodils had begun to bloom yellow, heads turned skyward. Soon they would be gathered and draped over the Easter altar, but now they covered the temporary grave of his sister. It had been a parody of beauty.

But now, in the quiet of the night, laughter skipped along between the barrows as a slender figure stepped into the moonlight. The pale blue dress they'd buried her in looked grey and misty now. She still wore her bedtime slippers.

"Come find me!" Nia called over her shoulder, and before he could respond, she was off, running between the graves, quick as a hare.

Rhys followed. But this time he gained on her.

She grew closer as his longer legs won out, as she pranced, almost leisurely, as if inviting him to win this game of tag.

He ran forward, hand outstretched, waiting for the moment his fingers would close around her arm, touch her shoulder, whirl her around to face him. But just as his fingers came within reach of the back of her dress— she leapt forward and vanished like a swirl of steam, dissipating in air.

Rhys stumbled to a halt, his surprise and momentum sending him tumbling to his knees, his outstretched palms biting into the hard-packed earth. He stayed on all fours for a moment, chest heaving, mind whirring.

A sob crawled its way up his throat. What was the meaning of these visions? Why here and now? What could she be trying to—

His eyes migrated upward. His chase had brought him right to the entrance of the burial mound, and now it loomed over him, eclipsing the moonlight and casting its shadow over his prone form.

While most of the old barrows had no doors anymore, they'd fashioned one for Nia's, lest vermin invade her resting place.

And now, that same stone stared blank-faced at him, greeting him with the same indifference as it had this spring. He'd wept before this stone. Beat his fists against it. Spent hours with his back pressed against it as if somehow he could convince it to relinquish the girl inside.

Now here he was again. But Nia's casket no longer laid in its confines. She'd been interred at St. Asaph's, along with the rest of their kin, in a proper grave with a headstone, and a proper Christian angel to guard her. So why was he *here?*

Nia had jumped through the stone, as if entering the barrow once again. Did she want him to follow her beyond, deep into the confines of the earth? What did she have waiting there? Is that where she could speak to him, in the dark of this underground place, once thought to be the touchpoint between this world and the other?

"You're mad," he breathed to himself. He'd thrown all caution to the wind and followed these phantoms in reckless pursuit, but this threshold gave him pause.

Nevertheless he shuffled forward on wary knees, and placed his palm against the familiar stone. He took a ragged breath in through his nose.

"Come find me," Nia had said.

Did she mean in the graveyard at St. Asaph's? Well, wouldn't she have led him there if she did? Though her body no longer lay in this barrow, did some part of her spirit linger here?

"You're *mad,*" he breathed again, as if saying it aloud would halt the dangerous thought forming in his mind. But even as he said it, his fingers curled around the rock as big as his torso, and with a grunt, he rolled it aside.

A cold air wafted out of the mouth of the barrow, as if something deep within had sighed. But there was no stench of rot, or even the wetness one would expect from a cave. It almost smelled...like springtime?

His muscles moved at half-speed as he lowered himself onto his belly. He knew, in some far reach of mind, what a daft thing it was to do— to stick his face in a hole in the ground at night, muchless the mouth of a *grave*. But that part of him, the cautious part, was subsumed by a ravenous curiosity, and a body that instinctively *moved*.

Soon, his neck was inside, his eyes stared into the blackness beyond. It was unfathomable, deep. Even the crags of the ceiling and the narrow sides were lost in shadow but a hand's breadth from his face. But wafting out from within was the unmistakable smell of *flowers*.

A laugh met his ears then, as if it were coming from the bottom of a well. As if coming from within. "Come find me!" Nia sang.

Rhys hesitated for just a moment. Thoughts of getting swallowed and pressed to death in the darkness swarmed him. But hadn't he already, in his own silent, solemn way, been buried alive for months? Hadn't he already died time and again and wished only for his body to follow suit?

Nia had told him to come find her. He hadn't been fast enough last time— but maybe he could be now.

So he wriggled forward into the dark tunnel, snaking along the floor on his belly. Soon all he could hear were his own grunts and ragged breaths. The passage was narrow, and he was thankful now for his lack of appetite these past months. Perhaps when he had been fuller, healthier, such a descent wouldn't have been possible. They'd only managed to wriggle Nia's coffin into the tunnel by shoving it from behind with the long poles and a sort of sling made of burlap. They'd never moved Nia's coffin beyond the first few feet, for fear they'd be unable to extract it when the time came.

How deep the tunnel went and for how long, he had no idea. But soon his own body blocked the light from outside, and all around him was darkness.

If he stopped moving, a panic and a claustrophobia rose to suffocate him. So he merely wriggled on. He was too far in to backtrack now. He must make it to where the tunnel opened into the burial chamber beyond. Then he'd be able to turn back. But for now he could only go forward. Chapped fingers scrabbled at dirt, cold air licked at his face, and from deeper down the tunnel— a laughter and a murmuring as if a little girl were singing to herself.

One of his shoulders burst through first, and then the other, and suddenly he was pulling himself out of the tunnel as if exiting some otherworldly womb. He sat up, hair brushing the ceiling. It was so dark he could not see his own hands, even as they combed the grit from his beard.

"Nia?" No reply graced him.

The only sound was his own breathing, loud in his ears. All ghostly song or laughter had ceased. His hand migrated to his pocket where his pipe and matchbox lay. He struck a match, the smell of sulfur close in these quarters, and then— a flare of light.

It took him a moment, eyes blinking against the sudden intrusion, to parse out the details of his surroundings. The barrow might've been larger once, but the walls pressed in close on each side. There was no sign of any previous occupants' bones— perhaps they'd sunk under layers of shifting earth, or were concealed from the weak light of his matchstick.

But his breath caught in his throat all the same.

Lying on the floor before him was the gleaming white of a mare's skull, and with it a tightly bound bundle of daffodils.

Rhys stared at them for so long the matchstick burnt his fingers. It fell to the dirt, winking out, and plunging him back into darkness.

He lit another with trembling hands. But no, his eyes had not deceived him. He crept forward on hands and knees, and examined the skull first. It was completely intact, picked clean, and ready for him to take home. Had some fox stolen it from his pasture and dug its way in here, his quarry in tow?

A fox might make sense were it not for a bundle of yellow flowers, fresh and virile, looking up at him from the floor. He reached forward tentatively, as if they would disintegrate under his touch.

But his skin met only smooth petals, stems wet with dew drops, as if just plucked from some spring morning. They weren't dried, like the sprig of Nia's funeral flowers Mam kept on her bedside table. These were fresh-picked. Impossible.

He scooped them up into his hands and the scent nearly overwhelmed him. He pressed them to his nose, to his cheek.

"Thank you…" It was all he could think to say. "Thank you."

His matchstick smoldered out, and he sat alone in the dark, drinking in the scent of those flowers— the first blooms of spring.

Each flower had meaning, his Mam had told him.

Aloe for affection. Amaryllis for pride. Lilies for purity and chastity. Palm branches for devotion and martyrdom.

Daffodils for resurrection and rebirth.

Daffodils for forgiveness and love unending.

Great, rending sobs shook all of him. Great gasps swelled and died unheard here in the depths of the earth. Great cries he had not let himself cry until now.

And each cry twisted a bit of his self-hatred free until the fragments of it fell like dead matchsticks onto the barrow floor. So many times he'd come to this barrow to whisper *'I'm sorry's'*, and *'please forgive me's'*. But now there was only one thing left to say, only one thing he *could* say:

"I love you. I miss you."

And he trusted that wherever Nia was, she heard. Whether it was here in the darkness with him, or in a grave down by St. Asaph's, or in a spring-time valley where the light never died and the daffodils never wilted, she heard him.

When he wriggled out of the barrow and back into the cool night air, the moon and stars blazed with a brilliance his light-starved eyes had never beheld before. The whole silvery world opened up to him, glistening and dripping with jewels. His chest opened up to breathe the freshness of the winter air and his tears blurred the stars into dazzling, flaming ribbons.

Down the hill, the town was still awake. For it was Christmas Eve and there was no sleep on Christmas. Smoke plumed from chimneys, candlelight glowed around the edges of shuddered windows. And from the steeple of St. Asaph's, the bells began to toll.

His legs were cramped and cold, his fingers dirty and chapped, but Rhys felt none of it now. Instead, horse skull under one arm, impossible bouquet of flowers in hand, Rhys ran across the barrow field towards town and the waiting midnight Mass.

FOUR

spooky action at a closeness

MADELINE SHEPLEY

TWILIGHT STREAKS HAD JUST STARTED to chase the sun below the horizon as Josephine walked up from the mess hall to the WIYN 3.5 meter telescope. As she looked beyond the Quinlan Mountains into the surrounding Sonoran Desert, the reddening sun hung like a brightly polished bulb ornament, low on the boughs of a Christmas tree.

It's like the universe wants to rub salt in my wounds, Josephine grumbled. She tucked a stray dark brown curl behind her ear before putting her hand on the door that led to the control room. *Like the universe actually cares, Josephine. Get your act together. The sun doesn't need your permission to rise and set every day.*

As she strode into the room, she saw the sandy-haired forty-something telescope technician sitting at the computers that controlled the telescope. The room was mostly bland other than the computers. Its only other decorations were posters of some deep sky objects, some metal filing cabinets, and some portable kitchen gadgets.

He glanced over his shoulder at the echo of her hiking boots against the linoleum floor. His emerald eyes sparkled when they fell on her. "Perfect timing!" He pushed up the rounded glasses on his

45

nose. "The 'scope just finished taking all your calibration images and is all set up for you to take the science images."

Josephine smiled gratefully and stuck her hands in her pants pockets. "Thanks, Brandon. I appreciate it."

"No problem." His lips pressed into a line. "I'm just still shocked that you showed up to *actually* observe rather than remote observe today...it being Christmas Eve and all..." It was his turn for his hands to disappear into his pockets. "I thought you would've wanted the freedom to go visit fam—"

She winced as Brandon's words stabbed her aching heart, so she threw up a wall around it. *Not again... I can't explain this all for the third year in a row.* "I'd actually rather have the peace of the observatory to myself this year," she said curtly.

Brandon's eyebrows crinkled, and he scratched his head. It seemed that he was searching for an invisible trap he had unknowingly stepped in. "Sorry. I didn't mean to pry...I just thought it was curious, that's all."

Josephine bit her lip. *Maybe I should back off a tad. Brandon makes the telescopes run, and being on his bad side would not be good when I still have observing to do.* She forced a smile back onto her face. "No worries. I'll be fine. I got it from here. You can take off."

He cocked his head slightly, but he seemed to think better of probing more as a smile popped up on his face to mirror hers. Then, Brandon stood up and dusted off his cargo shorts. "Excellent. Well, you know how to contact me if issues arise."

"Have a good evening."

"You, too, Josephine. Clear skies, and Merry Christmas!" Then, Brandon slipped out of the room like a transient event.

Once Brandon disappeared, Josephine let out a sigh of relief and released the wall around her heart. *Finally. No one to bother me...* She set her backpack down by the chair he had vacated and then sat down. Then, she withdrew her observing notebook and flipped it open to her observing plan. *Time to knock out these dwarf galaxy observations.*

Josephine typed the right ascension and declination of her first object—an ovular splotch-looking dwarf galaxy named AGC 731448—for the telescope to slew to. She also typed in the filter name and exposure time, then hit enter on the command line.

As she heard the telescope whir into position, Josephine heard a ping from her pocket. *I thought that I had my notifications on mute. I can't talk to them right now.* She took her phone out to check her notifications. She saw that her sister Clara, her brother Liam, and her mom had all texted her in the last few hours. She read Clara's message first:

> Hey, girl! Hope you're not too lonely up at the observatory tonight! We miss you! Hope you get to take some cool space pictures!

The next text she read was Liam's:

> Christmas has been sad without you here. I hope you get a chance to stop by after observing! I wish you didn't have to work over the holiday, but if you're not too sleepy after observing, join us for Christmas Day brunch! Mom would really like that.

And there was a follow up:

> You can't hide from this forever.

The final message was from her mom:

> Hope you're having a good Christmas Eve up there on the mountain. I know the holiday won't be the same, but it'd be nice to have everyone together for the holiday. Stop by if you're able.

Josephine ignored the texts and set aside her phone as a pang of guilt and loneliness stabbed at her heart. *Christmas is too painful now.*

I'd just dampen the holiday spirits. At least here there's no one for me to bring down.

That was the last thing that she wanted to think about. It had hurt as much as it had been sudden, leaving Josephine a bit unmoored without her anchor. *You know, he would* want *you to go on observing.* She pursed her lips thoughtfully. *That's what he'd have been doing in the backyard tonight, anyways...*

She glanced at the computer and realized that the exposure had finished. She pulled up the raw image to inspect. Her eyebrows knit in confusion as she examined the image to see not a fuzzy ovular shape but the faint grayscale vestiges of a giant spiral galaxy. *That's* definitely *not AGC 731448...* She frowned, the arms of the spiral brushing the forgotten recesses of her brain. *But why does this look* so *familiar? I don't research spiral galaxies.* She scratched her head. *Maybe I accidentally typed in the wrong ascension or declination?*

Josephine compared what she had typed into the command line to the dwarf galaxy's coordinates in her notes but found no error. *Maybe the mount got stuck for a moment?* She scratched her head. *Guess I'll just have to reslew to my target...* She retyped the observation information into the command line and hit enter. *At least it was the short exposure that got messed up.*

After hitting enter, Josephine brought out her personal laptop to work on her lecture material for the class on extragalactic astrophysics that she would be teaching in the spring semester. She wasn't about to let all the waiting in observing go to waste when the observatory had decent wifi. As a bonus, it had the comfort of blissful silence, her only companion the dime-sized black spider winding down for its sweet rest.

Once the five minutes of the exposure were finished, Josephine pulled up the raw image for inspection. She let out a gasp of surprise as she saw the white of the dome's metal panels instead of the white on black of stars against the inky black of the expanding universe.

"Why the hell is the dome in the way?" Josephine muttered. "Brandon opened it, and it was *definitely* open for the last expos..."

The faint sound of grinding gears coming from above her head sent chills down her spine. "What the—?" Without thinking, she leapt up from her chair, dashed through the door, and stumbled up the red-lit stairs to the telescope deck. *Did the dome get stuck on its track? It shouldn't move by itself.*

As she reached the top of the stairs, she surveyed the white and blue octagonal walls of the dome. The giant Ritchey-Chretien telescope dominated the room, so she peered around it to see the dome's current position. To her surprise, the dome was no longer blocking the telescope's field of view. It was as if there had never been anything wrong.

Did Brandon forget to tell me that something was malfunctioning? she thought. She shook her head. "No. Brandon's too good at his job to forget that. I must be imagining things."

As if to deny her verbal musings, the dome's interior white lights strobed, casting brief but undulating shadows on the wall panels and telescope as if she had been teleported to a pulsar. The sudden flicker of lights caused a brief stab of pain, dragging a cry of surprise out of her.

Once the lights settled down again, Josephine stumbled back down the steps and swept into the control room. *That was spooky, and it's not even spooky season anymore.* The stars in her eyes from the flickering swam in her vision. *It's just me in the dome, so it's got to be a malfunction. That's got to be it. Maybe I should call Brandon...* When she reached the desk, she snatched up her phone and clumsily dialed Brandon's number.

"What's up, Josephine?" Brandon answered after the second ring. "Is something wrong? Normally, things wait three hours before they decide to break."

"Have you been experiencing any issues with the motors of the telescope or dome or with the interior dome lights?"

"No. Why? It was working perfectly fine earlier."

"Are you sure?"

"Yeah. Why do you ask?"

"Things seem to be going bonkers up here."

"What kind of bonkers?"

"My first observation didn't even image my galaxy. Then, the dome somehow got in the way. When I went to check inside the dome, the dome was out of the way of the telescope, and the interior lights flashed at me."

Her words were greeted with a few seconds of silence on the other end of the phone. "Josephine...it sounds like the telescope acted of its own accord... but they don't do that. They're not sentient." There was another pause. "If it would help, I could come back up there and see what you're seeing."

Embarrassment and guilt rose in her blood like a flush across her face. *He probably wants to be with his family tonight. I can't keep him from them any longer than I already have.* "You'd do that? I thought you were going to be spending the rest of Christmas with your family..."

"I still have time to turn around. I'm not that far away from the mountain yet."

"That doesn't answer my question."

"I'll eventually get there, but it is my job to make sure that things are in tip top shape at the telescope."

"Since I'm observing in person, I don't want to get in the way of you spending time with your family." She bit her lip. *Even if I can't bear being with my family on Christmas, I shouldn't keep someone else from their own family on Christmas.* "Can't you check on things remotely?"

There was a brief pause. "I suppose I can see if there are any error messages on my end, but are you sure you don't want me to come back?"

Josephine hesitated. *Things here have been strange...but like Brandon said...telescopes don't act of their own accord. He's probably telling the truth, and it was just my imagination.* "Yes. You can go. I'll keep observing and wait for your word."

"Okay."

"I'll text you if I find anything. Let me know if anything else strange occurs, okay?"

"Sounds good."

"Alright. Bye, Josephine."

"Bye, Brandon." Josephine hung up the phone and sat back down at the computer in a frustrated flop. She had this weird hunch he wouldn't find any error messages. He was too good at his job to have left things in shambles. She had chosen her path, and she was on her own. *Guess I'll reslew again, and see what happens.* She took a breath to calm herself and typed in AGC 731448's observation info into the command line again. Then, she sat back down. *It'll be fine, Josephine. Dad would tell you to make the most of things and roll with the punches. Mishaps happen all the time when observing.*

She pulled up her lecture notes again on her laptop. She was working on some slides about the Great Debate, and she smiled knowingly as she typed. *It's the perfect time to mention Andromeda. It's the best galaxy, after all.* She brought two images of the iconic galaxy into her PowerPoint for the class—one of which she had taken with her dad a few years back with her amateur telescope.

We used to observe Andromeda all the time with his old telescope in the backyard and while camping. She sighed. *I would give anything to do that again.* she mused, staring at the fuzzy elliptical cloud in the amateur image she had taken of Andromeda. A few tears rimmed her eyes and stung them. *I miss him.*

The grayscale of an image popped up on the screen beyond her laptop. *Get it together, Josephine. You don't have time to think about all that right now.* Josephine straightened up and pushed her laptop aside, so she could better examine her raw image.

But this image was strange, too. A big black silhouette eclipsed the star-strewn night sky.

"What is...*that?*" she muttered, scratching her head. She leaned forward in her chair to examine the dark shape. Her eyes traced the dark outline of the figure, but could not tell no matter how many times she traced the outline what mysterious interloper had stolen all her stars.

Has something gotten into the observatory?

Chills went down her spine as the idea that she actually wasn't alone hit her like a freight train. *What the heck could've gotten in, though? Surely, I would've heard something.* She chewed her lip. *Well, if it had come through a door, I would've heard that. Maybe it climbed through the opening in the dome?*

Josephine got up from the chair again and stepped outside of the control room, only stopping to grab her pepper spray–just in case. She didn't even need to climb too many of the stairs to the observing platform to hear a loud chittering above her. *What in the world is that noise?*

As she crept onto the observing platform, she saw a bat was hanging from the secondary mirror support. Four more were just chilling on the ledge of the dome opening, silhouetted against the night sky as if they were sitting around enjoying a leisurely cup of hot chocolate.

"Are you kidding me?" she shouted. "Shoo! Go away!"

The bats just stared at her as if she were a crazy person.

Josephine rapped her hand against the metal walls of the dome. "Go away! You don't belong in here! You're disturbing my work!"

They turned away from her and chittered among themselves as if discussing what to do about the crazy astro-intruder.

She ground her teeth and stomped back down the stairs to the control room. "Those dang bats..."

A memory slipped out of the inky depths of her mind of a camping trip in Saguaro National Park as a kid. She remembered that she, her parents, and her siblings had been clustered around a telescope when a bunch of bats had flown out of a nearby cave, swarming them as they took flight.

"Good thing we have flashlights!" her dad had exclaimed, dashing towards the tents. He returned with the flashlights, and they used the portable light to disperse the nocturnal creatures from their observing location.

Josephine blinked herself out of the memory. She exited the control room again and flipped the light switch by the stairs. The interior lights flooded the dome above. Then, the bats shrieked, their wing beats fading into the distance. As they faded, she let out a sigh of relief, glad that her optical interloper was nothing more than a few natural creatures of the night.

"Good riddance." she muttered. She flipped off the light again and reentered the control room. "Time to get back to work." Once she got back to the computer, she retyped in AGC 731448's observation information. "Fourth time's a charm...hopefully."

The next five minutes passed like she was floating in the endless void of space, trying not to imagine what else could possibly go wrong. She tried to focus on her Great Debate presentation, but her anxieties kept popping up to distract her—and most of all, the identity of the mysterious spiral galaxy from earlier.

Out of the corner of her eye, she saw the exposure pop up on the telescope computer's screen. She straightened up and prayed there would be no more interruptions to her observing schedule. "Please be fine. Please be fine..."

Unfortunately, the fourth time wasn't the charm. A giant spiral dominated the picture before her, drawing a string of curses out of her. "Are you *fricking* kidding me?" She put her head on the table in defeat. "What the hell is wrong with this observatory tonight?"

Josephine groaned loudly and kept her head on the table for a while, bemoaning the way her night was going. She spiraled in her confusion of the observatory's shenanigans. *Why haven't any of my images gone right? What's wrong with the equipment? Why do I keep getting spirals instead of dwarf galaxies? And why did that one spiral look so* dang *familiar...?*

A thought arrested her from the spiral becoming a death-spiral. *Dad would tell you to persist... if you persist long enough, you'll get what you want.*

The astronomer peeled herself off the table and typed the dwarf galaxy's observation info for the fifth time. "Please... please let this work this time." Then, exhausted from fighting the system, she laid her head on the table again.

After five minutes, she revived herself from her weariness to check the image. She pulled up the image to inspect it, and let out a shriek of annoyance. Around the edges of the image were streams of light washing out the stars nearby. "You've got to be kidding me." she muttered as she leapt out of the chair and ran outside the control room to find the lights in the dome blazing brightly. "At this rate, I'll never get my observing agenda done." she groaned.

But Dad would tell you that the night is young, and that the observing doesn't end until the sun peeks above the horizon, her rational side piped up. *So you've got to keep pushing through. He wouldn't want you to waste these clear skies.*

Josephine sighed and once again typed AGC 731448's observation info. She hit the enter key with definitive force, then put her head back on the table. *Here's to hoping the observation works this time,* she thought pessimistically. *The universe* really *seems to be against me tonight.*

When the five minute exposure was finished, she pulled up the raw image to check it and cursed. A spiral dominated the frame, and the dwarf galaxy was *still* nowhere to be found.

"What the hell?" she muttered. "Too many unexplained mishaps keep happening, and when I actually get clean pictures, it's not of my galaxy...it's a spiral."

Josephine stared at the spiral thoughtfully and blinked. "Wait...I keep getting a spiral *every* time." She immediately typed a few strings of commands into the command line and brought up the three spiral images side by side. The spirals and the skies around them in each image looked the same, so she then brought up the image headers of each image to check what the images' central right ascensions and declinations were. To her shock, those central coordinates were the same for all three images. She then compared them to the right ascension and declination of AGC 731448 and saw they were notice-ably different.

"That's strange... why didn't the telescope go to the right coordi-nates?" Her eyes flicked between the three spirals before her and blinked again. "But wait. These are familiar." She bit her lip. *Could it be?* "Hmmm...I *wonder*..."

She opened up a web browser and opened up the Aladin Sky Atlas and typed the image's central coordinates into the search form. Sure enough, a giant spiral appeared near the coordinates. Josephine clicked on the galaxy and saw that it was the M31.

Josephine's heart almost skipped a beat. *The Andromeda galaxy! No wonder it looked so familiar. I haven't observed it in a long time; I forgot that it looks so different through a professional telescope.* Her eyebrows crinkled. *But why would the Andromeda galaxy keep coming up in my images when I wasn't even trying to observe it?* Her heart skipped another beat. *Is it some sort of sign? Am I supposed to observe Andromeda for some reason tonight?*

In another tab of the web browser, she looked up Andromeda's right ascension and declination. "I wonder what would happen if I intentionally observed Andromeda..." She then took those coordi-nates and some other exposure details into the command line and hit enter.

She waited another five minutes in anxious anticipation. Her mind was too jittery to focus on her lecture slides, so she got up and paced the room back and forth until the exposure finished. Only then did she sit back down to examine the image.

When she pulled up the image, the Andromeda galaxy was there just like the other three images. But the new image still featured oddities. A bunch of pixels were oversaturated at the bottom of the image. *They're not usually oversaturated in such large quantities.* Josephine zoomed in on the image to see if there was a recognizable pattern.

As she zoomed in, letters started to form and then words. Once she had zoomed in far enough, she read what was before her:

Here we are as in olden days
Happy golden days of yore
Faithful friends who are dear to us
Gather near to us once more
Through the years, we all will be together
If the fates allow
Hang a shining star upon the highest bough
And have yourself a merry little Christmas now.

Josephine's eyes watered as she put a hand to her mouth. *Oh, Dad... I miss you so much.* She gasped. "Dad, are you here?"

The overhead lights around the room twinkled like Christmas tree lights for a minute in response.

She nearly jumped out of her chair in surprise before a smile unfolded onto her face.

"You've been here the entire time, trying to get my attention with the observatory mishaps, haven't you?" she murmured in awe, leaning back into the chair to enjoy the unexpected show.

As if in acknowledgment, the overhead lights flashed off and on once. Josephine made a noise that was somewhere between a cry and a laugh. She could almost imagine him standing there in flesh, nodding at her with that warm smile she so desperately wished still lit up the Earth.

"But *why*?"

The lights nearest the computer flashed three times.

Josephine glanced at the computer screen and surveyed the lyrics again. "Here we are as in golden days..." she read slowly. "Happy golden days of yore." Her heart skipped a beat before she surveyed the room, remembering all those star parties.

Observing until she could hardly keep her eyes open and him tucking her into her sleeping bag on family camping trips...

Staying up until midnight to glimpse the Andromeda Galaxy at its zenith on his birthday...

Caroling with her parents and siblings around the family telescope late into the night after the Christmas feast...

She blinked. "You want me to continue the Christmas observing tradition, don't you, Dad?"

The overhead lights twinkled ethereally, almost like the stars that had captured her imagination so long ago. They seemed to twinkle like that forever until they gently drifted back into their normal setting.

When they finally settled again, a smile lit up her face—the first in a long while. "Alright, Dad. You got it."

As she turned back to her observing, it felt like her dad was standing at her shoulder. And in that moment, she knew there would be no more spooky actions tonight.

The next morning, Josephine hurriedly shut down the observatory, downed a straight black coffee from the observatory cafeteria to ward off the sleepiness, and zoomed the hour back to her childhood home in Tucson. She knew she couldn't delay seeing her family any longer.

The hour passed in a flash; soon enough, she found herself sitting in the cactus framed driveway of her mother's house.

An uncertainty that hadn't been there since the previous evening gripped her heart. *What if it'll be painful?* Josephine fretted, but then she shook her head. *No. It'll be fine. Dad wanted you to do this. No time like the present.*

She extricated herself from the car and trudged up the sidewalk to the front stoop. She rang the doorbell, then waited for what seemed like an eternity for whomever would answer the door.

When the door finally opened, the first thing her eyes fell on were piercing green eyes—just like her father's. They were ablaze with surprise, then delight. "Jo—Josephine! You came!" He threw his arms around her. "You *came!*"

"Liam! Who's at the door?" came the wizened voice of her mother.

"Come here, Mom! Bring Clara!"

The patter of two sets of feet echoed down the front hall before two women joined the brother and sister in the doorway.

"Josephine! I missed you!" her sister Clara exclaimed, sandwiching Josephine between herself and Liam.

"I missed you, too," Josephine murmured.

"You—you should've told me you were coming, Josephine," her mother stammered in disbelief. "We would've waited to—"

"I didn't want to disturb you guys so late at night," she said.

"But why'd you come? You haven't been to a family Christmas in three years."

A small smile reached to her lips, and Josephine inclined her head to a framed picture of her dad near the door. Then, she held out an arm in the offer of a hug. "A certain someone thought it was about time we all be together for the holidays again."

Her mom stared at her for a moment, then rushed in to join the group hug. As they did so, Josephine could swear that she saw her dad's portrait wink at his family's renewed closeness.

a christmas corral

A FRONTIER FLORA STORY
ZEPHYR THOMAS

THE BITTER WIND howled through the dry valley, like a voice calling out for something lost long ago. Up north there were trees to stop the cut of those icy gusts, but out here on the prairie, there was nothing but dust and grass. High on the ridge, a Choyote let out a keening wail, making the dogs in the camp howl back a warning. *Stay away,* they said. *This is our herd of Cloverhoof, and we're prepared to protect it.*

As the chill deepened, one of the cowpokes around the fire ring put on another few logs. Everyone else scooted a little closer to warm their bones. Three of the men wore matching blue flannel shirts; that was all the tailor had on hand when they ruined their other ones running away from a flood of molasses. But that's another story.

The shorter fella with a round face strummed on a banjo. "Home, home on the range!" he warbled. "Where Lavendeer and Cantelope playeee!" He made sure to hit that high note real high. "Where seldom is heard—"

"Aw, shut it!" the fourth man around the fire cried back. He stood out from the others for not only being a sight older, white hair and thick beard, but also for his plaid woolens. "You sound like a Purrsnip in a room full'a pruning shears."

"Hey," the banjo player drew himself up. "I thought the song says there weren't no discouraging words out on the range."

"It says *seldom*," said the man with the brightest eyes and the neatest mustache. An Ace of Spades stuck in his hatband, a bullet hole right through the middle of the pip. "Ed, you know what seldom means, don't you?"

Ed strummed his banjo as he thought. "I don't think we've got any doms to sell, do we?"

Ace leaned back in his seat, whistling.

The old fellow wasn't done yet. His Florabeast seemed to stir up at his agitation, a shiny Wartermelon curled up at his feet. "I'll be discouraging when I needs to be. You're gonna wake the dead with all that confounded yammerin'."

"That wouldn't be no surprise," said the last fellow, the tallest one even when they were all sitting down, his voice as deep as he was long. "It's nearly Christmas, after all." Before Ed could even ask what that meant, he kept talking. "That means, it's a time when the ghosts of our dearly departed come back for a little visit. There's so much celebratin' that they can't keep away. Everyone wants to be in on the party."

"I've heard as much, Boone," Ace said. "Say, speaking of Christmas, Doc Wilson is puttin' together a collection for the orphanage, treats for the kiddos and toys for their Florabeasts. Since it was just payday, we're in a good spot to help out." He put his hands on his knees, leaning forward. "I'm putting in fifty cents, what do you say, boys?"

Boone shook his head. "Payday was last week. You mean you just cleaned up at the card table again." Ace grinned that rakish smirk he was so well known for. Boone held out a dime anyway. "That'll make them littles so happy, I reckon." A bright red Ferradish hopped from Ace's lap, all rough, spiky ears and thick whiskers. It took the coin in its mouth then scurried back to its planter.

"I don't know, Ace," Ed said. "I just had to pay for that bridle repair, you know how my Muleein loves to chew through them..."

"Don't worry, Ed, I heard they need volunteers to help out too. You could get up like Father Christmas, giving away all the goodies, and..." he leaned in closer. "Miss Lizzie would be get up like Mother Christmas."

"Well pull me from the oven and dip me in honey, that's the job for me!"

Ace turned to the last member of their campfire vigil, the eyes of the Ferradish glinting along with his. "What about you, Sal? Care to put in a nickel?"

Sal didn't answer with words, instead doing something he could only do when no ladies were about, his spit sizzling into the fire. "What do they need our money for? I worked hard for my dollar, and that's what those pups need to learn too. You cain't just expect people to take care of your problems."

"They're orphans," Ace said patiently. "There's only two of the boys and one girl that are of workin' age, the others are still learning their three R's. They have all those mouths to feed and—"

"And what do I care?" Sal snapped again. "When I was young, everyone worked, soon as they could walk. Always somethin', even for the smallest to do."

Boone spoke up. "You ain't young anymore, old-timer."

"Haw!" Sal stormed away from the fire, his Wartermelon slowly coming to its hooves too, its shiny black tusks glimmering in the firelight. Its roots made popping noises as they retracted to find another spot to spend the night.

"That's better," Boone said. "Keep on playing, Ed."

Ed didn't, holding his banjo but staring into the fire. "I just can't believe the gall of that fella. Why does he have to be such a Gobblin about it? Not even a nickel? And at Christmas, of all times..."

Ace just sipped his coffee while Ed worked it out. Boone stared up at the stars, deep in his thoughts too.

"...He's acting like nobody ever did anything nice for him neither. I just... Why, somebody ought to teach him a lesson!"

"Hmm..." Ace looked up and rolled his neck around. "That sounds familiar."

Boone pulled himself away from the night sky. "How's that?"

"Reminds me of a book I just read, about an old British fellow. He was rich as the hills, but meaner than the dirt underneath 'em. Wouldn't even give a Christmas goose to his hired hands or sugar water to their Florabeasts. Took the work of some ghosts to get him scared straight again."

A log in the fire collapsed, sending up a shower of sparks. Ed jumped, shivering though the wind wasn't blowing that hard. "G-g-ghosts?"

Ace narrowed his eyes. "Yeah... I'm gettin' it all together now. I think this'll work. So listen, Ed, run over to the chuckwagon and ask Morris for the leftover flour from today's biscuits. Then, get the sheet off of your bed, and..."

The boys moved closer to discuss their latest caper. "Then when Sal comes back, you..." Their voices hushed under the sound of the fire crackling away, the wind rustling along, and the Beetbats whistling to each other overhead.

Sal came back to the fire from wherever he'd been. Might've been fuming over how there was no justice in the New World and how freeloaders were ruining things for everyone, or might've just been to the privy. Either way, he found the benches around the ring empty, neither the men or their Florabeasts. His Wartermelon was settled down outside the bunkhouse with the other 'beasts, stubborn enough not to move again even for its planter.

"No matter," he said aloud as he sat down alone, "it's quieter anyhow without that consarned banjo. Those boys, I swear, always up to no good."

Just then, two of those no-good boys were peering around the side of the pay office, the nearest wooden building to the fire ring. Someone had hung a banner over the door, a traditional Christmas symbol of a Hollyhawk carrying a Mistletoad in its talons. Boone wanted to light up his pipe, but he didn't want to risk giving away the game just yet. "You think he's gonna remember everything?" he said to Ace.

"Naw," his partner replied, eyes still on the fire. His Ferradish clung to his shoulders, looking around every which way to squeal as soon as it saw someone coming who wasn't one of his planter's best friends. "I know he'll forget most of it, but it ain't all that important. Just so long as he gets the big parts right."

"If you say so. I still think I should've done it, I can be the most imposin' when I needs to be."

"Sure, but Ed's the best with voices, Sal would just know it was you as soon as you opened your trap and—hold up, somethin's happening."

At the fire, Sal was still muttering to himself. A noise made him look up quick, peering into the dark to see if it was just one of the dogs, or something worse. It'd been quite a time since a Gast had gotten onto the ranch, but if one had, they had more to worry about than losing a few chickens. Even a slow little Jelly could make them worry about losing a few men. Sal's hand went to his revolver, checking to make sure he had enough salt bullets loaded.

There was the noise again, a scratching, scraping, something. Not much supposed to be in that direction, just the stock tank for the horses, nobody should be over there at this watch of the night. Sal gripped his iron courage, but kept it in the holster in case it was one of those darn fool boys playing some kind of trick again.

Clatter, crash, draw, pull back the hammer, stare into two glowing eyes...

Feline ones. It was just the camp cat, a scruffy old tom that was always chasing away the Pamplemouses and Ratscallions from whatever corners they were hiding in.

"You good-for-nothin' varmint!" Sal yelled, jumping to his feet. "Nearly gave me an apoplexy, get on with you! I don't care they named you General Washington, I knew the man and he would never sulk around in the dark like that!" He considered firing a shot, but didn't want to waste the bullet. Besides, it would send the whole camp running to see what news came with the report.

He turned back to the fire and nearly had that apoplexy after all: a pale, hunched figure stood opposite the ring, covered in white clothes that shimmered in the flickering firelight. Probably a man from how stocky he was, with a round face you could hardly see through all the glowing rags. Atop his head was one of those old tricorn hats, the kind only Beavirch trappers up north wore nowadays. He said nothing, just staring across the flames at Sal.

"Well I'll be," Ace whispered, "Ed did a boss of a job on that costume. See how he made the sheets glow like that? Must've run down to the creek for some Mistletoad slime."

"Huh," was all Boone had to contribute.

"Sal..." the figure wheezed. "It's been so long."

"You..." Sal's face was as white as his visitor's clothes. "It can't be."

"But it is. There are things you have to know, the rest of your short life depends on it."

"My what?"

"All our lives are short, but yours most of all. I was given leave from the Feast of the Departed to try and warn you. Your life will be over soon, and if you don't change your ways, this will be your ultimate fate—"

The visitor looked like he threw something in the fire, it flared up tall in bloody reds and punishing oranges. Sal took a step back, clutching at his heart.

Ace snorted. "Say, he was complainin' about money earlier, but that kind of fire powder costs a dime at the gastrologer's."

Sal blinked, shook his head. When he looked again the visitor wasn't across the fire, he was right beside him, staring him down. "The gold, Sal. You know where it is, and what to do with it."

Both Ace and Boone were silent, their ears open.

"That... the gold that we stole from the Royal Army?"

The visitor just nodded.

"Well, you know where it is, why don't you go get it yourself?"

"The Feast of the Departed ends on Christmas Eve, and I lack certain..." it stared at its rag-wrapped hands, "requirements to do the job. Besides, I am not the one who has lived hoarding it these past sixty years. Your whole town could have benefited from its use."

Ace licked his lips. "Enough gold to build a whole town?" Boone rapped him on the head to keep him quiet.

"Find it, Sal, and use it. You have many sins weighed up against your soul, but this will do much to help you in... the long run..."

"I... I... alright." was all Sal could muster.

The visitor walked back around the other side of the fire, gone back to its normal size and color. Just before he passed into that spot where you can't see something through the flames, he smiled. "Merry Christmas, and to all a good night." It stared directly at the boys, causing them to shrink back in case Sal looked that way too.

He didn't, breathing shallow and slumping down on the nearest log bench. "Mother of vinegar, I cain't take any more. Up in that gully," he mumbled, "should still be there unless someone else found it first.... too long in years to dig for it myself, but I cain't trust no one else." His hand went to his heart again, as though he could keep the rest of his time inside and not let it spill out. "I better wake up the Padre and get shriven, in case I keel over on the way." Sal got up and hobbled off away from the fire, slower than usual.

Ace was fit to be tied, about ready to keel over himself. "Gravy and biscuits, can you believe our luck? I don't know how Ed knew all that about the gold, maybe he'd heard a rumor or three and decided it was worth a shot. Anyway, Sal keeps his donkey in the west pasture, tomorrow morning let's have you send out your Min'talon to follow him, then we'll know whereabouts to search ourselves. Now just as soon as Ed gets back—"

"Here I am, Ace," Ed barely got out, breathing hard. He had his bedsheet rolled up in a clumsy pile under his arm.

"Say, how'd you get cleaned up so fast?" Ace said, ruffling his very flour-less hair. "I'd say you jumped in the stock tank to get all that flour off, but you ain't wet."

"That's just the thing," Ed took another second to calm down, his face red and flushed like he'd been running. "Old Morris was all out of flour for the day, that's why we had cornbread at supper. I got my sheet but then I thought to ride into town to Miss Lizzie's bakery for flour, but even my Muleein knows that she'd be heartbroken if I didn't stay for Christmas tea. You'd be out here all night for nothin'. So we're gonna need a different plan, since... hey, why are you two so done up?"

Ace and Boone had gone still, chills running from their hats to their boots. Boone had enough breath to speak first. "You mean, you've been running all over the ranch for flour, while—"

"Yeah, that's what I said."

"So you weren't around the fire, just now?"

"No sir, I didn't want to try to scare old Sal in just a bedsheet, he would've seen right through me. Or, I guess, right through it, at me. Anyhow, what's this all about, Ace?"

Ace's eye was twitching. He was supposed to be the calm one, imperturbable. Right then he looked mighty perturbed. "So you didn't hear a rumor about Sal's gold and try to get him to tell you where it was?"

"Gold? What gold?"

Ace started shaking, then crossed himself, Boone doing the same. Just then, General Washington hissed above them at some critter or another. Ace's Ferradish squeaked in surprise, and its planter made his retreat, Boone at his heels, headed for the relative safety of the bunkhouse. "No thanks, no cursed Redcoat gold for me!" Ace called out.

Ed was left outside behind the pay office, holding his bedsheet, an even more confused look on his face than usual. "Well, I'll be dipped. Guess I'll be having tea and cakes with Miss Lizzie after all."

The bitter wind howled through the dry valley, a voice calling out for what was lost long ago. That night, some dreamed about gold, some about dessert with a fine lady, and some about the long and dusty trail toward forgiveness. Putting the shovel to the earth might be the last thing he ever did, but if it meant he could punch his ticket for the happy home, he'd give it a shot. He'd work off the debt of his soul just the same way he worked off the debt of his flesh, with sweat and grit.

Besides, he wasn't really alone; Wartermelons were real good at digging, and his donkey was still stout enough to carry that moldy chest, even as full of regrets and memories as it was. Wouldn't Doc Wilson be surprised to see a contribution like that? There was always a chance to turn your horse around back towards the sun, especially at Christmas.

death doesn't make mistakes

BEN STAPLETON

THE CONSTANT TICKING of the grandfather clock irritated Gertrude. Sometimes. Most of the time it faded into the background, the same way the buzzing of flies did while gardening. Or how the irritation of her skin from the bedsheets fell away when she didn't think about it. But deep within her, pulsing with the tick of the second hand, lay something she tried to bury. Despite her best efforts, the pain was still there. It always would be there, until her last moments, but she could let it fade into the background if she focused on something else.

Rose-painted walls held framed photographs of all four of her children, along with one of her and Mortimer's wedding day. A bookshelf stood against one of the walls, though she couldn't read any of the titles without turning her head. Likely some of Mortimer's history books, or William's science-fiction novels that he still had to move into his two year new apartment. Five chairs lined her bed. They were the ones from the dining set Danielle, her daughter, made during a woodworking class. Mortimer's dozing form was in the one on her right, and one of her sons – either William or Albert, she couldn't tell in the dim lighting cast by the Christmas tree in the foyer – was sprawled across the two chairs on her left. She thought she saw her eldest son, Albert, standing in the shadowed corner of the room. But when she blinked there was nothing but the long shadow of the clock.

She licked dried lips with a parched tongue and croaked, "Mortimer, dear, can you get me some water? Spending a week this close to the veil has me parched."

He jerked his once copper, now dull bronze-covered head up. As he rubbed sleep away from his eyes, a tender smile touched his face, "You're awake!" It sounded a little slurred.

"I see you've taken no time getting your sleep in," she berated him. "Now can you be a love and get your poor old wife some water?"

"Will and I have been taking shifts. Well, all of us have been. Making sure somebody's here with you. Seems we both were too exhausted. But we took time to decorate together, like we always do." He gestured to the garland on the windows, the candles on shelves, and the nativity set on the bookshelf.

It was fuzzy, but she remembered hearing voices and the tinkling of ornaments. She also had a notion of the beeping of an oven and the scent of cookies. She smiled, hoping the scene was as joyful as she imagined.

"I'll be right back," Mortimer said as he spring up.

"Oh that boy doesn't need encouragement in his poor sleeping habits," she tried to call after him, but her voice only carried far enough to stir the sleeping form of William.

Mortimer returned with a fresh glass of water—no ice and lukewarm the way Gertrude liked it. He helped her sit up and drink. Gertrude grimaced at the need for aid, though she was grateful for Mortimer's silent understanding. Asking for help was worse to her than needing it. Her languishing joints were stiff, and creaked when she moved. Her face was scored with dozens of wrinkles, and framed by hair so white that snow looked dull in comparison. "I feel so ... so frail," she wheezed.

Mortimer smiled at her. A genuine, broad, toothy, goofy grin.

"Don't look it to me. You are just as mesmerizing as when I said 'I do'. The wrinkles add depth to you, same way a brook cuts a gorge through a forest to make it all the lovelier." He clasped her bone-thin hand and gazed into his wife's face.

She smiled back at him. Gertrude knew she always glowed in Mortimer's eyes, just as his gnarled hands holding hers reminded her not of the wizened man beaten down by the world. They were gentle, but strong. Just as capable of embracing her as they could shield her from the terrible things of the world. "But..." He trailed off.

"I know. These old bones are withering. How's Danielle handling everything? I hope she's not overwrought."

"Hasn't gone home to her apartment for weeks, she's either at work or here." Mortimer bit down on the last word, the way he did when there was something he needed to tell her but didn't want to.

"Mort, dear..."

He ran his fingers through his thinning hair, "Well, and I guess it's not just you she's been worried about."

"Dark and cold days, eh?"

Mortimer met Gertrude's eyes, and she could see the hollowness that crept into them this time of year. "I've been handling," he said, his voice creaking. "But these days are hard, thinking of Veronica out on a day like this. Then I start to blame myself. If I'd been easier on her, maybe she'd—" He choked back a sob. The silent hiccups racked his chest for a few minutes as Gertrude patted his arm with her own feeble hand. She wished she could properly embrace her husband, but the rot inside would flare and burn if she squeezed too hard.

"Mortimer. It's not your fault. Veronica was – is – an adult. She chose this."

"I just wish you could talk to her one more time. I wish we knew if she was even alive!"

"But I might not get to speak to her again. And we might never know if she's alive. And I know how it eats at you, but you can't let it sink you."

Mortimer was silent. The clock's ticking matched the beating of their broken hearts. Hearts that had lived in step together for thirty-odd years.

Their silent commiseration was broken by the draped figure of her son bolting upright. The young man, always slightly bewildered, rubbed his eyes and yawned. Gertrude couldn't help laughing at William and his ability to both sleep and wake at the least opportune moments.

"Oh, Mom! You're up!" Her son showed a smile just a little more goofy than Mort's. Gertrude's laugh devolved into a cough. Mortimer patted and rubbed her back while William's face darkened, and a helpless look crossed his face. "Mom?"

She waved him back as the fit subsided. "I'm alright, dears. Just got carried away. Say, William, how have you been? It feels like ages since I've been well enough to hold a conversation."

William's face twisted up in worry. His eyes flicked nervously towards his father then back to his mother. "Well, I sort of found a new job, working as an editor for an online publication." Seeing his father's face, William quickly added, "But I didn't leave the mill for this! It's a part time gig—I work in the early mornings before my shift."

"Well I'm glad you're doing something with your writing." Gertrude sent a pointed look towards Mortimer. Mort nodded, his face blank.

"Not my writing. Other folks'. But I'll learn what I can from this job." William had a sheepish look on his face, "And I can build my network - find an agent - maybe even get my latest book published!"

"Another novel! My, that's your fourth!" Gertrude put all the excitement her weak body could into the words. William getting excited about work was a true treasure. Rare and, to her, priceless.

"It's. Yeah. Another one." William glanced nervously at Mortimer, who gave a reassuring smile. Or it would have been if the corner of his mouth didn't twitch downward. "It's about a girl that goes missing. I—I know how hard it was when Veronica left. Maybe it can help others. Or just for closure, for us. Something we can tell ourselves about where she went. That she lived a long and happy life. Unfortunately, I just haven't figured out the ending." A car door slammed outside, and footsteps crunched in the snow.

Mortimer sprung up from his chair. "That must be Danielle. I'll help her bring in the groceries."

As her husband exited the room, Gertrude reached a shaking hand out to William. He clasped her hands in his. "How long have you been working on this one?"

William looked off into the corner of the room, his eyes seeing miles passed it. "Ever since..." Gertrude wiped away a tear from William's face, the same way she did when he was young and first scraped his knee, or got hit by a baseball he hadn't seen, or later that week when he was told he'd need glasses the rest of his life.

"Since she left?" Gertrude was tearing up now too. "My William. In want of a heart big enough to keep everyone else safe inside. How did your father react when you told him? Assuming you told him before now."

"I told him last week," he cast his eyes at the floor now. "He didn't seem bothered by it. But maybe it just made him sad. I hope not."

"I'll talk with him about it. I'm sure he's just overwhelmed with..." She gestured at herself, "But I'm glad you're willing to remember your sister. Your father might just think you're saying she's never coming back."

"Sometimes there are only whispers left of us. And sometimes the only sign any of us were here is the stories we tell. I don't think dad understands that I'm trying to keep her alive, rather than saying her memory is dead."

"I think it's a noble thing you're doing for all of us. Mortimer will see reason. He always does."

William beamed, then the shadows deepened on his face and he opened his mouth to say something else when the garage door slammed open. Rubber soles squelched on the mudroom floor as Danielle and Mort returned, carrying groceries in by the armful.

There was a crash as Danielle dropped hers haphazardly on the counter and dashed into the family room where Gertrude was. Mort sighed and set his down gently. He went back out for another load, smiling all the while. Danielle threw her arms around her mother, clothes wet from the freshly fallen snow and clinging to Gertrude's form. "Mom! I'm so glad you're doing better!" Danielle's greeting was somewhere between a laugh and a sob.

"I'm so glad to see you awake too!" Gertrude laughed, and a lance of pain tore through her chest. She cried out.

"Sorry! Sorry!" Danielle exclaimed, leaping back from her mother's frail form, her pale face flushed red.

"It's... ok." Gertrude wheezed out between coughs. With a shaking hand, she downed the rest of the water Mortimer had brought in for her. William took the cup from her and went to refill it. Danielle slumped back into her chair, eyes downcast. When Will returned with the glass Gertrude thanked him and gestured for him to join his father in the kitchen.

William's face passed from confusion to understanding, and he nodded. "You need help with dinner, Dad?"

"Sure, can you get the carrots and potatoes?" His father called back. Will gave his sister a hug, his mother a smile, then whisked away into the kitchen.

Once the two were given some privacy Gertrude asked, "Why so sad?" She cooed the way she had when her children were young and dealing with the trials of growing up.

Danielle raised her eyes to meet Gertrude's. "I just feel like its all on me."

"Like what? My illness?"

"It's..." Danielle gestured at the room around them, "everything. I'm worried about Will not taking work seriously, I'm worried about Dad being too hard on him, I'm worried about Albert getting lost in chasing money. And yeah, I'm worried about you passing away."

A lump formed in Gertrude's throat. Not out of anger or indignation, but love and hurt for how she couldn't help her daughter. She knew how the illness felt. That creeping pain. Icy claws reaching for her heart. It hadn't been a decision to stop fighting it. The outcome became inevitable. "But - but I'm here now," Gertrude said.

"I know. Just why this? How can I fix it? I know I can't, so why can't I accept it? I just want to be able to help you, Mom!" Danielle's voice rose as little beads of glistening water formed at the corners of her eyes. "I want to have an answer."

"My Danielle, who could always solve any problem. Sadly I don't think we get to know the specific why behind everything until we're on the other side of death's door," Gertrude smiled wanly. "But I do know that there is *a* reason for it all. And sometimes not knowing it gives us time to grow to where we can appreciate the truth of things."

Danielle drew in a shuddering breath, "That's hardly any consolation."

"No, but maybe we shouldn't worry about making the world what we want, but learn to accept it as it is."

Danielle tightened her jaw at that. "There's also the fact you're aware right now. I'm happy to see you doing well, and it could be a sign you're getting better. But..."

"But what?"

"But there are also a lot of cases of folks getting a lot better just before they pass." Danielle said it quick, like the sounds being in the air for less time would be less painful. The clock ticked. Was that Veronica standing in the corner now? No, it had to just be the shadow again.

Gertrude shook her head, her eyes must be going. "Oh." Gertrude said, the knot of pain inside growing angrier. "Well if I am to go, us sulking about it won't help any." Gertrude clasped the side of Danielle's face. "Not to say I don't appreciate your concern, but let's enjoy each other's company, tears and all, without making things more sour."

William called from the kitchen, "Dinner's ready!"

Mortimer set up tray tables for each of them, and William and

Danielle brought in the cumin roast carrots, mashed potatoes pulverized to nearly a liquid, and baked chicken that was the wrong side of dry.

"This looks delicious! I can't wait to see what you two make for Christmas dinner this year," Gertrude said as they sat down to eat.

"Aren't we going to wait for Albert?" Danielle asked.

"I gave him a call while we were cooking, but he said he can't get away from the office right now." Mortimer's voice had a touch of acid to it.

"Did you tell him Mom's up?"

"Yes," William snarled. Then he saw Gertrude's face and relaxed. "But he's focused on a big project right now. Said he can't get away."

Danielle's face turned red and Gertrude's heart sank. Before Danielle could say anything Gertrude spoke up. "Well it's his own life. I'll just have to see him later. Let's pray!"

Solemnly they prayed. They ate with only small conversation about their days, none willing to mention the missing party. When the dinner was done and dishes cleaned they sat gathered, laughing over jokes and listening to Mortimer pluck his old guitar and sing. Danielle's shoulders loosened up for the first time Gertrude had seen since she stopped her treatment. William had a genuine smile on his face, and Mortimer's eyes were a little less distant. When William went off to bed, excited to get to work tomorrow for the first time in years, and Danielle was asleep in the guest room, Mortimer sat for a time with Gertrude. The clock ticked.

"Mortimer dear," Gertrude began. "William told me about his story."

"Yes." Her husband's shoulders drooped a little.

"You know he's not writing it to condemn you, even though you want to be condemned. He's writing it for all of us. To have a memory of Veronica. I wish I could read it, but I don't think I'll see the day it's finished."

Mortimer clutched her hand, wary to cause her more pain than she already felt. "I ... I know he means well by it. But we don't know she's dead. We just—don't know. It's just a reminder of how we – no, how I – failed Veronica. I put too much pressure on her, and that's why she hasn't come back or called. That I'm the reason not all of your children are here for you." He broke into tears then. The silent kind that didn't stir the dead.

"It's hardly your fault Albert chooses money over family. And I'm just as much to blame for both." Gertrude rested her head back against the bed and closed her eyes. "I just have one request for when I do pass, Mort. Read William's book. Consider it your Christmas gift to me this year. I know you'll still be good for our family, but please read it. I think it might help you to look at her leavetaking in a new light."

Mortimer nodded his head slowly. The two sat in silence for hours, simply happy to be near each other. The clock ticked away.

The grandfather clock chimed in the corner of the room. Midnight. Moonbeams peaked in through the windows, and a dimmer eerie green light came from the pine-filtered lights of the tree. A glass Mortimer had been nursing after dinner sat half-full on one of the trays. Open on one of the chairs sat a book William had been reading —a collection of Edgar Allen Poe's writing. The wind picked up outside, squalls blowing the freshly fallen snow into a drift. A lonely car drove down the street, shadows thrown from its headlights danced across the wall. The light flashed across Gertrude's eyes and the clock chimed its twelfth chime. Then the bell clanged a thirteenth time, stretching beyond its normal length, becoming a jumbled cacophony that filled the room. Ears ringing and eyes stinging, Gertrude lay dazed for a moment. Then the world fell silent. Like creation itself had drawn breath.

The harsh white of the headlight gave way to a soft blue moonlight that washed over the room. Suddenly a well-dressed man was seated in one of the empty chairs. He wore a fedora over a bald head.

The pale skin of his face looked to be stretched too thinly over his skull. His eyes were solid black, with tiny flickering flames where the pupils should be. His suit was ash grey, and a purple tie of thirteen knots was looped around his neck.

Gertrude's heart leapt at his ghoulish visage, "Wh-who might you be?"

"Oh you know of me. At least, you've heard of me before."

"I must be hallucinating. Or dying." She laughed. A hollow sound, like wind passing between dead trees. "Well at least the second of those is nothing new."

"Yes, you are dying. But this is no hallucination." Those solid black marble eyes bored into hers, and the flames seemed to dance with each beat of her heart. Hungrily.

"I don't see how this isn't a hallucination, you hardly look like how I'd imagine God to look, or the devil for that matter."

He leaned back and laughed, "No, no. I'm not Him. One of my coworkers tried to be Him once and it didn't go so well. I'm just an old friend of humanity's."

"So you're the Grim Reaper?"

"Ah, not quite. He's technically my boss." The man said, leaning in conspiratorially. "and let me tell you, he's a real taskmaster. Works us to death half the time, and never gives any rest to the wicked."

Gertrude looked at him blankly, though her heart was racing. "So what's your name?"

The man leaned back, adjusted his suit, and doffed his hat. "My apologies, madame. Where are my manners? The boss always says first impressions are the most important, and mine are always the last. Well, except the poor tailor that made this new suit for me." He flicked his cuffs and adjusted his tie. "The fellow looked like he'd seen death. But I promised he wasn't on my list. Yet. I am called Roberto, the Psychopomp. Pleased to make your acquaintance." He bent then and brushed bone-dry lips against the back of her bone-thin hand. "Most stories about those in my trade paint us in quite the dour light, and I've done us no services here. I'm here to guide you across the veil, ferry you across the rivers Styx and Lethe, and present your soul for Judgement on those Eternal Scales."

"So you can't make it any less painful?" Gertrude relaxed. The pulsing flames in Roberto's eyes slowed to match. The pain was still in her chest. Her lungs worked like the bellows at William's steel mill. She could hardly lift her arms. But deep inside she felt no worry or fear. At least, none for herself.

"Unfortunately not. Dreadful thing, souls being torn from bodies. Used to not happen this way until old Louis got jealous and vengeful. True shame, that, especially as exquisite a thing the body is." The flame in Roberto's eyes flickered and dimmed and he spoke in a small voice. "Makes me a little jealous, if I could feel such a thing as jealousy, that I should never know what it's like to taste the air or hear the sunrise."

Gertrude laughed. "For what it's worth neither of those would do you much good, the air can only ever be tasted when it tastes foul, and I suspect if I'm ever close enough to hear the sun I'd be burned away."

"Really? Well maybe I'm better off as I am, if I can't do those things I really would like to do." Roberto put his hat back on his too-smooth head then continued, "But while I can't offer you physical relief, perhaps I could assuage any fears you have? Most folks are far less calm when the process starts then you are now, but I can still offer what I may."

Gertrude racked her brain trying to think. If she were to pass, maybe she could offer something for Mortimer, Danielle, Veronica, and William? Perhaps she could learn... "Say, you mentioned a list? How does that work, may I ask?"

"You may ask even if it were forbidden for me to answer. Fortunately for you, this is one question I am allowed to answer." Roberto reached inside of his coat and procured a long roll of paper. Or rather, the end of a paper because it trailed into his coat regardless of how much he pulled. The paper was dry and crinkly, it smelled of a cabinet too long left closed and neglected. The ink was faded to little more than a stain. Written in crimson were hundreds of names, places, dates, methods of death, and so on. He pointed to a name. "Here is your entry. 'Gertrude Isabelle Amarie, December 16th 2014. Fairhill, Maryland. Organ failure due to cancer.'" There were other names too, up and down the page but none she recognized. Most were dated for this day or the next.

"And can I ask if someone's been on the list in the past or will be there in the future?"

"Eventually everyone is on the list. From kings to shoe shiners, accountants to engineers. What's a little messier is telling you *why* someone is on my list. See, we have a strict non-intervention policy. Other spirits can speak to mortals, but it's not in the Bureau's charter. Not since one rash psychopomp chose to shuffle some paperwork and caused a whole mess of a day. Folks didn't die who should have and the whole thing became a mess."

"Why would people not dying be a bad thing?"

"It's terrible when you've been decapitated," Roberto said soberly.

Gertrude shuddered and deflated a little. "So you can't tell me when you might pay someone a visit?"

Roberto winked at her and said, "I never said it's a no. Just that it's messy. I can show you an entry, but I can't tell you anything more than what's on the list. And if you try to tell anyone. Well, let's just say the walk was even more unpleasant than normal for the last one who did. Now, who do you want to know about?"

"Could I ask about my daughter, Veronica? She's been missing for quite some time and I'd just like to know if she's still alive."

"I haven't heard of that name coming across any of our desks, though I am fairly new at the job. I'll see if I can find her name." He began pulling the list out of his suit. It collected on the ground in a tangle like the weeds Gertrude would pluck from her garden. So many names Gertrude never knew—could never know on this earth. All spooled out before her eyes as simple lines on a page. She didn't have apprehension that Roberto and his ilk were there to hasten anyone's death, but it dawned on her the sheer size of human tragedy contained on that page.

At last, after what felt like years had passed, Roberto held before her the dread page. One end sticking into his suit, and the other disappearing in a knotted mass on the floor. Where his nearly skeletal hand pointed she read a name. *Veronica Rose Amarie Stephenson; July 18th, 2067; Anchorage, Alaska; Stroke.* Gertrude's heart leapt. She might be able to heal her family yet! If only she could leave a message. "Is she there now?"

"I said I can't answer that. I can only tell where everyone has their final moments, not the path that lead them there." Roberto's eyes grew distant as his pupils of flame shrunk. "I've seen mere slivers of so many lives."

"Do you know if she'll die alone?" Gertrude's voice caught.

"I can tell you that everyone dies alone in the strict sense," Roberto gestured to the empty room around her, "Do you see any others around you right now? No? But would you say you feel alone? Unloved? Like no one cares for you?"

Gertrude shook her head. "I don't feel alone."

Roberto nodded. "'Course not. It's usually a door that only ever opens for a single soul at a time, unless there's a grand tragedy. I don't mean to sound harsh, but even if you were to pass while others were here, it's a thing you experience alone. Or at least it would be, if I weren't here. And on the other side ... well you'll see it soon enough." He turned his gaze on her then and smiled as warmly as an icy spirit could. "I know that's not what you were asking. But I can't directly answer that question. If you ask about others of the same last name I can show you their entries."

Gertrude composed herself and asked, "Does anyone by the surname Stephenson pass around the same time?"

"I can tell you there is another death a few years later with the same last name as hers. One Vincent Alexander Kolbe Stephenson."

"Do you carry messages to those you guide?"

"Depends on the message."

"Can you take a message to Veronica, whenever you might cross her path, that we will always love her, no matter what?"

Roberto nodded. "I'll do it, if she still hasn't reached out to your family by her passing."

"I thought you said you can't tell me about what happens in the lives of those who pass after me?"

"I can't, you're right. But I can speculate." The spirit winked at her.

A warm bubble formed in her chest. "Can the list change?" She would do one last thing for her family before she left them.

"Of course! Humans have free will and take actions every day that shorten and lengthen their time on this earth." He pointed to a name three feet down the page from Veronica's, and before Gertrude's eyes the date shifted to two months earlier. Then the name disappeared, the name below it sliding upwards to take its place.

Gertrude struggled to lift her hand then, and reached for the book splayed open on the chair next to her. With trembling fingers she grasped it and dragged it onto her bed. "Well Roberto, do you mind respooling your list so my home is tidy for my last moments? You know it's rude to make a clutter in your host's living room."

"I'm sorry, I hadn't realized," he said sheepishly. "As you wish." He began packing the long sheet back into his coat pocket. Though as the yards of paper were shoveled back in, no change came to the thickness of his chest.

While he was distracted, she grabbed a pen from the bedside table and flipped William's book open. It was in the margins of a rendition of *The Bells* where she jotted down a note in crooked script. Curse her ailing hands! But it would have to do. A tear slid down her face and off the bridge of her nose, splashing onto the page and making the letters look fuzzy.

With that done, she closed the book around the pen and held it to her chest. The pain racked her whole body now, and she could feel her spirit tearing free from her body.

Roberto glanced up and pulled out a pocket watch. Gertrude couldn't read any of its symbols. "Ah, it's happening now. Remember to breathe. Your soul doesn't need oxygen, but the act helps keep you focused on something. Or so I'm told at any rate."

The burning that had been steadily rising within her finally reached a fever pitch. The agony reached deep to her bones, a pain worse than any she'd experienced before. She thought of learning to ride a bike as a girl and scraping her knee. How she wailed over that small injury. Then of the ordeal that giving birth four times had been. How happy she was when she cradled each child. She remembered when she first was diagnosed, and the painful procedures that followed were all worse than what she had lived through before. All of that together was nothing compared to this. And yet the pain now was more bearable for the experiences she'd had. And unlike those hurts, this experience was done in moments. Then she stood without pain, looking down upon her lifeless body clutching William's book. No translucent form or wispy sheet trailed behind her. "I guess you can't believe all the movies about ghosts, huh." She laughed, the sound like wind chimes on a summer evening out in her garden. It filled the house for a moment then it was gone, and she heard a door slam open upstairs.

Roberto stood then, and gestured towards a doorway that had appeared beside the grandfather clock. Its ticking had resumed, though it sounded fainter. More distant. Less real. "This way, Madame. I can walk with you a while."

"One moment," she said as she heard footsteps rushing down the stairs. Mortimer ran into the room where her body lay, he felt for breath from her nose and a pulse on her wrist. He found none. Cradling her body, silent sobs racked him. Gertrude's spirit knelt beside him and embraced him. She kissed his cheek and whispered, "Lead our family as you always have, my love."

Mortimer lifted his head and turned to face her, his lips parted and ready to say something, but his eyes didn't focus on her face and looked right past her.

Then Gertrude and Roberto set out through the doorway, and Gertrude passed on from this earth.

Nine days later Roberto reclined on a branch in the tree of the backyard of the same house Gertrude had passed in. He wiped oily sweat from his brow with a bloody and charred sleeve. Immolation was a terrible way to die, he decided. He pulled out his list to verify he was at the right address. If his flawless memory served, it was here, and Roberto liked to memorize the list two weeks in advance. With his busy schedule, he rarely had the time between visitations to update beyond the next name or two. Out of curiosity he searched for Veronica's name. The address had changed to one in Fairhill, Maryland, just a few houses down the street from this one. He cracked a toothy grin. More than one name changed since the night Gertrude passed. His next appointment wasn't here any longer, and he'd have a long time yet before he'd return to this home. Wearing a smile fit for a skeleton, Death stepped off to greet his next patient.

white elephant

KELLY GROSS

THE *DINGALING* SIGNALING the start of the company "Holiday Winter Extravaganza" sounded on Max Kincaid's computer. He smiled, ready for it, not just for the free Mexican food that he could smell from down the hallway, but for the White Elephant exchange. It wouldn't be long now and he'd be rid of it. Rid of *it*. He'd be free, and set to go back to his normal life without the white ivory elephant statue. Rid of its voice whispering next to him. He wouldn't need extra blankets at night to stop him from shivering. He'd be able to type without feeling like his fingers would crack at the slightest movement. No more pin pricks of ice as he moved. People wouldn't ask if he was sick because he wore two extra sweaters or wobbled as he walked. He wouldn't hear its voice in his head. He'd be free.

"You're going to give me away?"

He heard it below his desk, in the bag that he had bought at the Dollar Store along with the tissue paper he had stuffed into the bag over the statue, hoping to drown out its voice. It didn't. He looked around his cubicle where Jeannie and Issac stood, chatting with the people over their shared wall. They hadn't heard anything, they hadn't heard it all morning. The voice was Max's burden to endure alone for just a little longer, just until he could give it away. It'd be someone else's problem then.

Sasha looked at him. "You ok, Max?"

"Yeah, yeah, just ready for the party. You?"

Sasha smiled happily, always chipper. Too chipper if you asked Max, but she was nice enough and she did her job, so he couldn't hate her. "Oh I'm always ready for Christmas celebrations. We've got this one and then tomorrow, my friends are taking me to what they call the Christmas Crawl, have you ever heard of it?"

He nodded. It was a bar crawl held downtown where singers sang on the street and cheered passersby along. Then everyone participated in a drunken parade at midnight. "Yeah, it's fun, but I haven't done it in years."

"Well, I can't say I'm much of a drinker, but my friends say there's other stuff to do too."

"Yeah, McClanahan's has some games and karaoke times if you're into that."

Sasha's eyes widened with excitement as she nodded, "That's what I'm going for."

"Just stay clear of Damien's Bar." Max added.

"Oh? Why?"

"Bad management. Don't want you and your friends to get involved with that."

"Good to know. Thanks, Max."

McClanahan's was owned by an old Irish gentleman who still managed to have the accent and brewed his own beer in the back. It tasted awful, but it was cheap, and that wasn't the reason to go anyways. The reason one went to McClanahan's was to either eat the famous crack dip or to hook up with a stranger. That's where Max had found her, on Black Friday, just a few weeks before the work party.

Max sat on the old red leather bar stool. He had been drinking with his buddies, but they'd all left one by one until he was alone. Some went home to their wives and children after a generous helping of chips and dip. Others picked up women who had come forward and flirted with them until Max was nothing but a nuisance. Max didn't mind; after all, the tall blonde in the corner booth had been smiling at him all night long. He lifted his glass to her, and she slunk over.

"Hello, your friends left you all alone, I see."

"I guess they're not really my friends then, are they?"

She smiled, showing off her pristine white teeth and sat down on the stool next to him, crossing her long legs. "Well, maybe I can be your friend, then."

"I won't complain."

She laughed and looked at the chips on the bar and slowly picked one up before popping it into her mouth and seemed to wait for Max to say something else. Where were his clever words? Did he need clever words? Obviously *she* had approached *him*, so he might have won already. "I haven't seen you around before."

"Haven't you?"

"I would have noticed."

She tucked her almost snow white hair behind her ear. "I suspect that's true. It is my first time here. I normally go to Damien's, but it was closed for an infestation, according to the Health Department."

"Well good, I'm glad planting those rats worked, then."

She laughed like a jingle bell—soft but strong—and he felt an urge to get her to laugh again. "I must say the clientele here is very welcoming."

"They weren't at Damien's?"

She shook her head slightly and bit her lip. Whoever had been cruel to her there deserved great punishment. "Well don't worry about it. Plenty of good folk here."

"Good folk?" She asked, teasingly, her eyebrow raised.

He could feel his face heat. Right, that turn of phrase was odd. He shrugged, trying to play it off. "My dad used to say that all the time, never really got rid of that."

"Hmm- well, nothing wrong with that." The barkeep came up to ask if they wanted anything else to drink.

Max looked at her. "Would you like something? My treat."

"Not here," she said, smiling, reaching out to caress his hand, and then led him out the door.

Their boss, Debbie, stood by the door in a set of lighted reindeer antlers, holding a Santa hat filled with numbers. "You can put the present on the table, Max. And take a number. Happy Holidays."

The rules of the game were simple. Everyone in the department brought something that they no longer wanted around their own house and was at least something of a little value. If it was trash, then you were expected to have a gift card attached to it. The statue was valuable, it had to be, though Max hadn't been able to get it examined. It *looked* valuable at any rate and so it passed the first test.

He reached in, digging around in the hat and grabbed a folded piece from the bottom. Quickly he glanced down at the number: *Twenty-Six.* There would be three or four people after him, and his bag should be long gone before that. Max smiled to himself as he set down his gift bag in front of the other presents and went to join his cubemates at the long conference table.

Max, Max, Max. You wanted this. Don't you miss me? Why are you doing this?

It whispered to him across the room, but still no one heard it. Issac stared at him, a confused look in his eye. "Aren't you going to get food, Max?"

Max looked at the others that were already seated, their plates piled with tortilla chips, tacos, salsa and rice. Right. Food. He did need to eat. He smiled, "I am, just wanted to set my stuff down." He put his bottle of water in front of him along with his phone and joined the line near the food table. *Come and get me, Max, it isn't too late.*

He ignored it and tried to focus as the new guy rambled on about how his old job didn't have parties like this, and how the background Christmas music would have been banned, especially the "Baby, It's Cold Outside" song. Max didn't have the heart to tell him that it probably was banned, but none of the Department cared that much. A bunch of Christmas songs weren't on anyone's priority list here. But maybe that was what the new guy meant.

Max piled a heaping of rice on his plate and flour tortillas before adding on the spicy meat, hoping that it would alleviate the chill that grew in his bones. At the end of the row, he took an extra small plate and took two of Sasha's gooey brownies before they were all gone. They always went fast, and on another day he would have already snuck one or two in the cubicle he, Sasha, Jeannie, and Issac shared, but he had been distracted. As per usual of late. No one at the office had commented on it other than a 'vacation hasn't started yet, Max,' when he didn't answer a question fast enough.

She hung on his arm all the way to the car, smiling at him, teasing him. He unlocked his doors and opened it for her like a gentleman. He let her pick the music— some Christmas pop tunes. He let her convince him to sing different songs like "Winter Wonderland" and "Run Run Rudolph." Max then realized she hadn't been singing at all and said as much.

"Oh I don't have that particular gift."

"It only seems fair if you sing too. Come on, every kid learns a Christmas song. Pick one. How about 'Away in a Manger?'"

She wrinkled her nose at that and frowned. "No, no. I'll do 'Jingle Bells.'"

She then proceeded to sing. Horribly. Somehow sharp and then flat and then sharp again. Max regretted not taking her word for it. Soon enough, she was done and he said something like 'thank you.'

"I told you it'd be terrible."

He laughed at that. "So you did."

"So now, you owe me one."

"I didn't realize that that was how it worked."

"Well, you should learn to ask more questions then," she said, running a finger along his arm.

Max smiled, playing along. "Well then, what do I owe you?"

"I want you to sing me this song," she said, as the familiar notes to "All I Want for Christmas is You" washed over the speakers.

"Oh no," he said, chuckling. "Isn't that overdone?"

"Nonsense. It's very catchy and popular for good reason. I'll just keep playing it over and over until you concede. Besides I know you know it. Everyone does."

He had to give her that. At the stoplight he looked over at her, her face glowing, happy. How could he disappoint her? So he motioned for her to start and he made it through the whole song, mostly without laughing.

She had been a fun night, joking, laughing, teasing each other. It was only in the morning when he felt the cold ivory trunk of the elephant statue around his finger that he noticed anything odd.

You said that I was all you wanted, Max. Don't you remember?

"No," he said and Jeannie turned to look at him, an odd expression on her face. "Sorry, just thinking."

"Well don't think too hard, it's Christmas," Sasha piped in. "What's everyone's plans?"

Max shrugged as the others took up the conversation again. Ski trips, family Christmas, people still had to get turkeys even though it was only a few days away and the volume of shoppers would be terrible. Max glared over at his gift, ready for it to talk to him again, though she remained silent for the moment. When would they get started? They all had their numbers didn't they? What was the holdup?

"And Max?"

He looked up to Sasha with her young wide eyes. "What?"

"What are you doing for the holidays?"

"Haven't decided yet." He shrugged his shoulders. Christmas was usually a lonely affair since his parents were both gone. He didn't go to any church. His friends had their own families and while he was invited to their houses, it always felt *odd*. Like he didn't quite fit there either. So he usually read, got Chinese food, and went for a walk.

Jeannie stared and said, "You say that every year."

"Do I?"

"Yes."

At first, Max thought leaving the statue of the elephant the size of his hand in bed with him was a clever way to get him to come find her. He went to McClanahan's the next day and waited the entire night, but she never showed up. Disappointed, he had gone home alone, back to the elephant that he'd placed on his nightstand. Maybe she had just gotten busy with something. Maybe she was playing hard to get. He couldn't be sure of anything.

He hunkered down in his bed and pulled up his sheet, ready to turn on the TV and fall asleep to it, but instead, accidentally grabbed the elephant at first. It was cold, colder than it had been that morning and he nearly dropped it. Setting it back down on the nightstand he looked at his hand, it was red where the statue had been, tingling, and Max wrapped his bedsheet around it, hoping to warm it up. This time he more carefully grabbed the television remote and turned off the light.

He slept and only awoke when he felt a cold drip on the back of his neck. Max sat up and felt for it, only there was nothing there. The television now showed some lady trying to sell a fancy ermine earmuff, and Max turned the channel. He must have dreamt it. Rubbing his neck again to reassure himself, he snuggled back down into his bed, hoping to get to sleep again quickly.

The next day was worse. His hand that had felt frozen the night before now felt like it was being pricked by a thousand needles when he moved it, the only solace appearing when he held a cup of coffee, which he ended up doing the whole day. Luckily it seemed no one noticed. After work he went to McClanahan's again, but again, she didn't appear. Grumpy and wired from all the coffee he had earlier in the day, it was more difficult to go to sleep. When he did, there were no drips of cold on the back of his neck. Instead, it was as if someone took an icicle and kept tracing his skin over and over, searching for the best spot to puncture him. Max moved to the couch to no avail, even though he wrapped himself in blanket after blanket.

As he sat there, feeling the cold seep into his bones, he decided to get rid of the elephant the next day.

Finally, only one person was still picking at their food and said that they shouldn't wait to start the game. The first few gifts were chosen, some blatantly breaking the rules by having new things, but no one called them out. His bag still hadn't been chosen as the numbers rose past fifteen. People were opting to steal already opened gifts rather than open a new gift themselves. He sunk into his chair. Maybe he could disappear into the floor. Maybe he could run out of the room and just "forget" that he needed to choose a gift. What was he going to do if he couldn't actually get rid of it?

The first thrift store refused to take the statue on account of it being made of ivory and they were against animal cruelty. Max tried to tell them that it was an older statue, made before it was illegal. That only prompted them to ask for provenance which Max could not give. Max didn't think that he'd be allowed back at that thrift store any time soon.

The next store had a drop off bin that Max could set the statue in and leave without talking to anyone. He did, quickly turning back to his car, barely noticing that the radio only played Mariah Carey in the background. He ate dinner happily and it was only when he headed to his bedroom that he noticed in the corner of his eye the elephant sitting on his nightstand once more.

"I got rid of you."

Oh Max, you didn't even say goodbye.

Max felt his heart hiccup for a moment. It had found its way back and was talking? No, no, no. He whispered to himself. "No, it's just my imagination."

Oh Max, you know it's not.

He didn't answer, backing slowly out of the room. The next day he'd take it back, say goodbye, and be done with it.

That didn't work either. It didn't work to dump it in the trash or give it to someone on the street, and every night his skin prickled at the cold as he shook under the covers.

They reached number twenty-six and his bag was still on the table. Max walked slowly up, ignoring the thundering rush of blood in his ears. How had no one chosen his bag? There were only three gifts left. He chose one in a green bag, knowing that it could be stolen. Still, he hoped for something bad only for his heart to sink when it turned out to be an unopened bottle of scotch with glasses. He could only hope that it wouldn't get traded with the statue.

On the eighth day of trying to get rid of the statue, Max walked back into McClanahan's hoping that she would be there to explain herself and he could finally be rid of it. People were beginning to notice that something was off with him. He shook the new guy at work's hand the day before and the new guy had commented on Max needing to warm up. They were starting to comment on him shaking as he handed them sheets of paper. Not to mention the strange looks he'd get when he didn't respond to something quick enough. Jeannie had asked if he hadn't gotten enough sleep when he couldn't remember where he had saved a report that he ran every day. Isaac asked if he was hungover when his speech started to slur as they practiced a presentation. Something needed to change - quickly.

He sat back down on one of the stools and waited, but only Patrick McClanahan, the short balding owner, paid him any heed. "Max! You're back, and I have just the thing for you to try."

"Is it warm?"

"Warm? I don't have many things that are served warm, but this will surely warm ya right up. Give ya a bit of a kick in the teeth, too." Patrick said as he poured whatever concoction he had made up in front of Max and expected him to drink. Max downed it quickly, waiting for the sting of alcohol to warm up his body. It lasted a few seconds before the cold shadow settled back over him.

Max tried his best to smile at the kind man, but Patrick was furrowing his brow, studying Max. "That was good, Patrick. Thanks."

"Ya don't need to be patronizing me, Max. I know when ya like something or don't. Now, tell me. Something's troubling ya, your smile isn't reaching those eyes of yours."

"It's complicated. You wouldn't believe me."

Patrick smiled and leaned over the bar. "Oh, I've seen plenty in me time here, and I'll see plenty more. Tell me before ya go crazy over it."

Max hesitated, and Patrick poured him another drink. After that, the words came more easily and he explained everything as Patrick's face turned grim.

"And do ya have it here, Max? Did you bring the statue?"

Max nodded and reached into his computer bag to take it out and set it on the counter. "How do I get rid of it? Do you want it?"

"Oh no - I want nothin' to do with that. You can put it back now. Only two ways I know - one, get the fiend that gave it to ya to take it back. But since ya've said that ya haven't seen her, best go with the second."

"And that is?"

"Someone's gotta willingly take it - or steal it."

"I tried giving it to thrift stores."

"A thrift store isn't a person."

Max went home despondent until the next day at work when Sasha reminded him of the gift exchange.

Jeannie was next, and didn't even look at the scotch. Max relaxed a little. That was right, Jeannie didn't drink. She encouraged others not to drink. For a moment, Max worried she would choose his gift and he'd have to answer questions in a few days on why the statue was talking to her, but she seemed to have paid attention to what gift that he had brought and avoided that. Opening hers she smiled when she got a nice coffee mug with fancy grounds from some shop that Max didn't know.

"Isn't that what you brought yourself?" Sasha whispered to her and Jeannie laughed affirmatively and gestured to her to keep it a secret.

The new guy was last and got stuck with the statue, whistling as he pulled it out and showed everyone as people gasped. It did look rather shiny and expensive, Max thought as he saw it go into the hands of another. But that tinge of greed was quickly replaced by relief, then worry, as the person who drew number one got up. They were the last to steal if they wanted to - was it possible to still end up with the statue? No. No it wasn't. Even as the coworker walked towards Max and put the dancing avocado socks in his hands, taking the scotch for himself, Max couldn't quite believe it. He could go home. He could go to sleep.

There were a few more games with a few questions that Max had to field from the new guy. "This looks expensive, why do you want to get rid of it?"

"No, it's just collecting dust. It's not actually worth that much. Please, I want you to have it." Max said, trying not to lay it on too thick.

He hurried home, packing up his things for the long weekend. His head hit the pillow and he breathed out deeply, almost giddy. He had done it.

It was gone. The poor new guy had taken it, probably was going to sell it and really what did Max care about that? He hoped that the new guy could. If he were the type to do a jig, he'd do one.

As it was, he'd go and get a drink at the bar the next day. He could almost taste it, the bitter liquid coating his tongue while a haze drifted over him. Max reached for his phone and sent off a quick text to his buddies about meeting up the next day for the bar crawl to celebrate. They didn't even need to know what he was celebrating. Pleased with himself, he put down his phone and turned out the light to get a good night's rest, only to hear next to him, whispering in his ear, *"Sleep well, Max,"* as a cold elephant statue's trunk wrapped around his pinky once more.

the reason

E.P. FUSELIER

I WAS A TORTURED MAN, and I had no salvation.

As a child, I never had nightmares. And I was never one of those kids who was afraid of the dark. It always seemed such a stupid fear. I mean, with all the other actual stuff to be afraid of— tornados, kidnapping, getting lost, car wrecks— the dark was an illogical fear. It couldn't do anything to you.

A belief I held onto happily and naively until thirty years old.

I wish I could go back to being a child. For now, as a self-reliant, adult man, the darkness plagued me. Even if I left a light on, something still lived in the shadows. Cackled in laughter just as I drifted to sleep. It enjoyed my suffering.

The first night, I thought it was my neighbor's damn kids. You would think with the amount of money I paid for this unit, the walls would be made of more than paper. It seemed I heard every little tantrum, every infuriating giggle. At this time of year, out of school on Christmas break, their noise was constant. But that first night, they shouldn't have been awake. I myself was falling asleep, that sweet spot where your mind is still working, but you might not notice if a three headed pig or something of the like floated by.

"Trying to sleep?"

I sat upright in bed, staring into darkness in wild confusion. The silence seemed to ring in my ears. I had heard a voice, right? I tried to replay it in my mind, to remember the sound of it. But the sense of the voice slipped away.

No, I must have imagined it. I was too close to dreaming, and I woke myself up. I thought maybe it was the neighbors, but there were no muffled voices from the next door apartment. The quiet was so complete, with no rustling, no disembodied breathing, no tick-tock ticking that I concluded it had been my dreams. The mind did strange things. Sleep paralysis, sleep walking, and so on.

I laid back down and closed my eyes. The more I settled into sleep, the more I was convinced that the voice was only in my dreams. As I drifted off, my mind latched onto the ambient sounds of the apartment— a creak on the ceiling above me, a faint door slamming down the hall, the building settling. But nothing was out of the ordinary and I fell asleep, unbothered.

I woke up later that night not knowing why. I had the sense that there was danger nearby. My heart was pounding. It felt like there was someone in the room with me, just beyond the sliver of ambient light coming from the street light outside. That was ridiculous. No one could be in my apartment.

The front door was locked. No one besides the landlord had a key to my apartment, and the last time a girl had lived with me was at a different place. There was always the chance that the landlord had been a cheapskate and never changed the locks. If that was the case, I'd sue his ass off. But I'd been living here for six months. If someone had the key to this place, why wait so long?

Reaching out to my bedside table, I fumbled for my phone, pulled out the charger and woke up the screen.

1:33 a.m.

Less than two hours of sleep. I swiped to the phone's flashlight and shone it around the room, just to convince my hammering heart that there was nothing to worry about. And sure enough, there *was* nothing. Just my desk, covered in mail, my laptop and various junk I had thrown down there. The chair in front of it held a mound of clothes, having taken its job from the hamper which sat useless in the corner next to a set of incremental weights that collected dust. At the far end of the room was the door to my bathroom, halfway closed.

I laid back down, determined to get back to sleep, and I did. But I soon woke again. And again. Each instance a jolt of confusion, a memory of a voice, a feeling of a presence in my room. Was this what it was like to have nightmares? That they lingered? I tried to convince myself that was what was happening: the residue of the dream seeping into my waking moments. But I didn't remember being scared when I was asleep. It was waking where the fear emerged.

After the second time that night, I tried some preventative measures. I searched my apartment, looked in every closet, but I was alone. I tried leaving the bathroom light on, turned on white noise from my phone— just in case it *was* the neighbors waking me. But still I continued to wake, the morning deadline creeping closer as I grew more anxious, knowing each time I woke, I would be that much more miserable the following day.

I did sleep a little, but it felt like nothing when my 6:30 alarm rang. It was time for work.

The next night, I fell asleep without meaning to. I woke up with a crick in my neck, the T.V. frozen on the ever concerned "Are you still watching?" screen. This time, I hadn't woken in a panic. Instead, it seemed my body simply wanted the comfort of my bed. I had come home from a miserable day at work, popped two more ibuprofen to chase away the headache that had plagued me all day, and eaten dinner in front of the T.V. Apparently, I had fallen asleep.

I rubbed my neck and squeezed my eyes with my forefinger and thumb.

Sighing, I sat up and began to stand, but froze. A dark figure passed across my bedroom door. Someone was in my apartment.

It was too quick and too shadowed to make out any kind of detail. But I could see that it was short, not like a child but certainly shorter than an average adult. That should have emboldened me; I was bigger and taller than whoever this was. But just the fact that someone was in my home had shaken what should have been an advantage. And then there was the way it moved. The figure's head turned toward me as it passed, as if inviting me. Or challenging me. It wasn't slinking, as if to hide from me. It was confident.

There was no sound from the room. No fumbling around in the dark.

I was halfway standing up as my panicked, paralyzed mind scrambled for defensive action. A knife— in the kitchen. But what if they came after me when my back was turned? I'd have to keep facing the doorway.

Slowly, I rose to a full stand and sidestepped toward the kitchen, making sure to keep facing the bedroom door. Nothing else moved in the darkness, but I knew what I had seen. After a few backwards steps, I made it to the kitchen and I reached my right hand out, groping for the knife block. My fingers grasped empty air. I flicked my gaze to the side, got my bearings and snapped my eyes back to the bedroom, half expecting a grotesque, long haired specter to have materialized in front of me.

But no such horror movie trope waited. My bedroom remained as dark and seemingly unoccupied as it should be. But somehow, this was worse, because I was still gripped by the suffocating antic-ipation.

My hand finally found a knife handle. I pulled it free and held it out in front of me. With the blade in between me and any would-be attacker, I felt some of the tension ease out of my shoulders, although my hand gripped the handle as a vise. I'd get that son-of-a-bitch.

Still, I waited, fighting the urge to call out to check if anyone was there. I didn't want to alert an attacker to my presence and I didn't want anyone to answer. As quietly as I could, I crept forward and arrived at my open bedroom door. From the light of the living room, I could dimly make out my desk and chair at the far wall. I reached out a hand along the wall and flipped on the light.

Empty.

Desk, chair, bed, dresser. I swung a look under my bed, but there were only shoes. The closest door was closed. Had someone gone in there, closing the door behind them softly so I hadn't heard it?

Quickly, in order to not give them the time to prepare, I crossed the room and yanked the door open, raising my knife in attack.

No one.

The only place left to check was the bathroom but I had seen the figure go in the other direction. Still, I checked but as before, it was empty. I was inexplicably alone.

I thought briefly about trying to find somewhere else to sleep but the idea of trying to explain the situation to one of my friends was enough to keep me there for the night. I mean, what was I going to say? That I had seen someone in my bedroom but they vanished? I had no desire to be thought of as crazy.

That night, I once again didn't sleep well, but this time it was because I couldn't quiet my mind. It took me hours to fall asleep, and I kept waking, expecting this time to find the intruder standing over me. The anticipation made me see shapes in the dark that were only illusions, and search for any sound in the silence. I both wanted to hear something, to prove that there was something to see, but I also didn't want anything to actually be in my apartment. My body was tense, my jaw perpetually clenched. I needed to sleep but I did not want to. I was vulnerable in sleep. Clearly this thing was choosing the moments when I was helpless.

At the end of the night, as the morning sun turned my room to a hazy gray, I was utterly exhausted.

Over the following few nights, it only got worse. One night I heard a voice, and I could have sworn it was singing "I want a Hippopotamus for Christmas" as it woke me. Which shouldn't have made me afraid, but there was a sense of mocking that sat with me, as if it could make even lighthearted things drip with despair. Another night, there were no sounds, but I kept seeing something out of the corner of my eye as I got ready for bed. And of course, every time I turned, there was nothing. I woke up with that feeling that someone was in my room. Another night, every single electronic in my apartment came alive. My T.V., my microwave, my oven, my PS5, and every light were on full blast, waking me up in alarm. The faucets in the bathroom and kitchen turned on as well. Some nights, it was a combination of all of these phenomena. After the seventh night, I was ready to do something about it.

I looked up ghost hunters near me but only found ghost tours, but the search engine helped refine my search to *paranormal investigators*. That felt a little pretentious. Still, I called them up. An older sounding guy answered and said he couldn't come immediately, and that it would cost seventy-five bucks. Then, when he got to my apartment, three days later, he brought in a bunch of electrical equipment that looked to be stolen from TSA. He took a lot of measurements in every corner of my apartment, none which he said showed signs of high energy. I had no idea if he was full of bullshit or if there was actually some science to his methods. Never before had I believed in ghosts or anything supernatural, but something was going on in my apartment. I had to hope that he knew what he was doing.

Whether he did or not, or whether this thing wasn't moved by his gadgets, I didn't know. The only thing I did know was that my apartment remained haunted. That night, various objects flew around my room. The mound of clothes fell off my desk chair, I jolted awake to the sound of a picture frame crashing to the ground, and heard the sound of tromping feet. I flicked on the light, raising a bat in my hand. A pair of my own shoes— black steel toed boots I had only worn once— sat in the middle of my floor. They had walked of their own accord from the back of my closest where they had been gathering dust. My fear and weariness fought each other. I was afraid, and I dreaded every noise I heard. But the lack of sleep was also rubbing me raw. I could feel myself starting to not care.

I moved to the living room and tried to get some sleep on the couch, choosing to keep with the T.V. on. I had tried the couch before, and I knew this thing haunted the whole apartment. But if there was already noise from the T.V., maybe I could stay asleep.

I got only a couple of hours of sleep, which I was grateful for, but nothing short of a full night's sleep would save me. This time of year, carolers were singing about silent nights, and how I wished for *that* Christmas gift.

That day, I called up a unitarian minister and got her to cleanse the place. She came after I got off work and walked around the room with a bundle of unlit sage and sprinkled the room with water from a plastic bottle labeled Holy Water. I asked her where she got it and she said the chaplain at the hospital she volunteered at. She said a prayer asking for the room to be cleansed and then lit a stick of incense.

It didn't seem like anything happened, and yet when she left, I was hopeful. It really felt like there was a chance I'd finally get some solid sleep.

That night, the laughing started.

Well, I never put much stock in the unitarians anyway. I mean, just pick a belief. If I was going to kick this stubborn thing out, I would need someone who had a little more conviction.

On the afternoon of Christmas Eve, fighting a pounding headache, I called up my buddy, Mason. He and I used to party together in college, but he went soul searching for a few years and then had a literal come to Jesus moment. Now he was a pastor at some touchy-feely evangelical church, and we occasionally got coffee. He kept the dates because he was always trying to convert me, or worse, invite me to his services. I kept going because it was a good time riling him up. Toe the line of blasphemy, and he'd get all indignant. But then no matter what I'd say, he'd always invite me back.

I didn't give him too much detail, just said there was something off in my apartment and asked if he could come say a few prayers.

"I'd love to help," Mason said through the phone. I held it away from my ear, far enough that it wouldn't exacerbate my headache. "But I've got church services tonight for Christmas Eve. Tomorrow we've got the big Christmas service, and then I'm spending the rest of the day with my family. I can come first thing on the twenty-sixth." That would be two days. I wasn't sure if I could last that long.

"If I'm still alive by then," I half joked. I didn't want him to know how worried I was about this, but if I didn't get real sleep soon, I wasn't sure how I could function. Even talking on the phone was making me see white through this migraine. "Is there anything I could do in the meantime?"

"Uh, maybe call a priest? They're usually on call for this type of stuff."

No, thanks. A priest would probably sense all the sin I'd been getting up to in my apartment and run away, clutching his pearls.

"Yeah, maybe I'll try that," I lied.

"And look, you know you're always welcome to join us at our service tonight or tomorrow. No obligation, no judgment. There's even some good coffee."

"Thanks," I said, willing to put aside my snark for today. He had done me a favor. "But I like to sleep in on the weekend."

"Alright man, but let me know if you change your mind."

I ended the call and stared at my bedroom. The night before had been intermittent with laughter, and I felt like I hadn't slept at all. Well if religion couldn't help me, I'd just leave. Even in desperation, I still stood by my decision to not tell my friends. But I could get a hotel room. It was going to be an expensive bullet to bite, as it was Christmas Eve, but I couldn't stay here another night.

I checked into the nearest, decent hotel for an exorbitant price. The lobby was bedecked in too many Christmas trees and garland, and the staff was too cheerful. Why? They were working on Christmas Eve.

Once up in my rented room, I quickly unpacked only what I needed in order to get in bed and then I fell asleep, my head nestled into the cushioned down of the hotel pillows.

For a second time, the voice woke me. I was sure it was a voice this time. No more wondering if I was crazy or if I had truly heard something. I *knew* it this time. But my foggy brain couldn't recall the words.

But that meant it wasn't my apartment that was being haunted. It was me. A nauseating fear rolled over my body. What could I do? Why was this thing following me? Why me? What had I ever done to deserve this? A sliver of anger drove away a portion of my fear.

"What the hell do you want?" I yelled out into the room.

Laughter came from a corner of the room and I froze. Unlike times before in which it seemed to come from the whole room at once, I felt like I could point exactly where the entity was.

"So he finally responds," said a voice from the corner. My heart hammered in my throat, so violently it felt like I might vomit. The voice was a little high pitched, but not feminine, nor child-like. Mocking. That was the only way I could describe it.

I scrambled for the bedside light and somehow found the switch amid my panic and blindness. I flicked it on and let out a gurgled cry of alarm. In the corner of the room, sitting in the hotel chair was a person. No, a creature. For although it looked humanoid, I knew this thing was not human. And I knew it was what had haunted me every night for the past week.

It was short, with a rounded head and jet black hair in an almost bowl cut. I couldn't tell if it was a man or a woman, but I suspected neither. It had a strange blend of both and what was even more unnerving, some sense of the face of a child. Wide eyes and smooth unblemished skin, a stubbiness to the fingers. But the way it sat and proportions of its body spoke of something older— much older once I considered the expression with which it stared at me. It wore a stark white shirt with a high collar and sleeves that came to a sharp cinch at the wrists. Over it was a deep red vest and for its pants, it had pants of an emerald so dark, it almost looked black. It had one leg propped up on the other so that its pointed, shiny black shoes made an impression of severity.

I clutched the covers to my chest, wanting to shrink into the pillows like a child.

"Come, come," it said. "A down comforter isn't going to do much to protect you."

It was talking to me, after all these nights of passively torturing me, it was casually chatting with me. I stared with my mouth open, unable to form a coherent thought. Too many questions battled to be the first asked, and without even consciously choosing it, I said, "What are you?"

If it was a demon, it certainly wasn't anything like I had expected. Demons wouldn't look so human, right? Maybe it was an alien? Oh God, was I going to become one of those crazies who claimed they had been taken in the middle of the night and probed by extra-terrestrials?

"Hmm, what am I?" it mused, a glimmer of amusement in its eyes. "It's a tricky question to answer because it's not something you have a basis for."

I frowned. "Are you a demon?"

"No," it said in a patronizing tone. "If I was a demon, that would be easy to explain to you."

"Are you an alien?"

It gazed at me with one eyebrow raised, like a cartoon character. "Do you want me to be?"

"I want to know what you are," I said firmly, annoyed it was avoiding the question. "And why you've been harassing me."

"What am I? What am I?" It steepled its splayed fingers then tapped them together melodically. "If the universe is a kingdom, I am a jester. If it is a circus, I am a clown. If it is a Shakspearian tragedy, I am a grave digger. If it is a basketball game, I am the costumed mascot who has hijacked the kiss cam." It smiled, baring its teeth which I saw to my horror were sharpened to points.

None of that made much sense to me, but I did get that it was a creature that liked to cause trouble. Even the way it talked wasn't straight forward, as if conversation were a game.

"The closest name you might have for my kind is an imp," it continued, "but I find the term inadequate and degrading. It certainly does not convey the dignity that the rest of my cousins have in their titles. But I suppose," it said in a pensive tone, "I have a different purpose than they."

It gave a dramatic flourish of its hand. "I exist because someone out there has a sense of humor. And I'm in your room because *I* have one."

My confusion was suddenly replaced by anger. "What does that mean? Why are you doing this to me?" I wanted to get up and strangle it.

"Because it's fun." Its eyes sparkled and it grinned, the points of its teeth glinting in the light of my lamp.

"Not for me," I said with vehemence.

"Oh, I suppose that's true." It looked thoughtful, as if the idea truly hadn't even occurred to it. As if I reveled in two weeks of no sleep. "So I suppose this is fun on your behalf. You're used to it the other way around." His tone indicated that he found this passively amusing.

"What?"

"Oh you know. All those people you harass on the internet."

I stared in wild confusion. "You're haunting me because I chew out a few idiots on Twitter?"

"No, that's not why. I just feel like it's poetic justice."

"Well, what did I do? Why now?"

"Because it's Christmas," it said, smiling at me with a wickedly mischievous grin. "Consider it a gift."

Right. I felt so fortunate.

"So what now? Are you going to show me my past and make me feel all guilty about how greedy and selfish I am, and I'll have a happy meal tomorrow with that little cripple's family on Christmas morning?"

"This is where the second game begins."

"What game?" I snapped.

He smiled as if being asked was the greatest pleasure in the world. "I ask you a question, and if you get it right, I leave you alone forever."

"What?"

"You like that word."

"But wha— you haunt me night after night, you won't let me sleep, I'm miserable and now all the sudden you just want me to answer a stupid question?" Frustration bubbled in my chest. I hated it, sitting in that chair as if it were my guest.

"Would you rather I keep *haunting* you, as you say?"

"No, It's just— it doesn't make sense."

"Oh ho, so sorry my actions don't make sense to your puny mortal brain." It stared at me and we sat in silence for a long few seconds.

"It's not a trick question, is it?" I asked. "There's a real answer?"

"Yes, there's a real answer," it nodded gleefully.

"And if I get it wrong?" I asked.

It shrugged. "I'll give you three chances."

"And what if I get it wrong?" I asked again, emphatically.

It gave a bewildered look, as if it couldn't fathom that was possible. "I guess we could find out how long a person can go without sleep until they start to hallucinate. A fun science experiment."

I ground my teeth. I didn't want to have to give in but this was my way out. And it wasn't as if there was another choice.

"Ok, what's the question?"

"What," he said, pausing theatrically, "is the reason for Christmas?"

What? That was it? That was the plot of every Christmas movie ever made. I opened my mouth to respond, but stopped. I found I couldn't nail down a specific enough answer. All those movies had the same general concept: Anti-greed, anti-capitalism, "it's more than the gifts," blah, blah, blah. AI could easily write one of these movies and no one would spot the difference. But to articulate this sentiment, I needed something more specific, not just what it wasn't.

I thought for a moment longer, then said, "It's about focusing on our family instead of the gifts we're going to get."

The imp raised its brows. "Oh, and if someone doesn't have family? No Christmas for them?"

I shrugged. "Ok then, family and friends." I certainly didn't talk to my family anymore but that didn't mean I didn't celebrate Christmas. There were plenty of parties I attended.

"And what if someone doesn't have friends?" it asked.

Was it going to find the most obscure exception to my answer? "Everyone has friends."

"Oh do they? Well, if you say so."

I huffed. "Fine. So that's not the right answer."

It smiled in confirmation. "Would you like to try again?"

"Yes," I grumbled.

"Alright, let's hear it. What is the point of Christmas?

"Good will and—" I shrugged. "Love toward our fellow man. Doing good works and all that." It wasn't the most eloquent, but I felt like it conveyed that saccharine message implied by the singing choirs and tinkling bells outside of stores.

"A good answer," it said, pleased and proud. Relief buoyed my chest, but the creature continued speaking. "But it's not the correct one."

What the hell? What did it want me to say? Jesus? Like those stupid bumper stickers on twelve passenger vans that said, "Jesus is the reason for the season"? Did this miserable, sadistic creature want me to say that some guy who got killed two thousand years ago was the reason we mindlessly over-consumed during the darkest part of the year in order to cure our seasonal depression? Did it want me to say that the biggest hoax ever played was the reason we used to get off for two weeks in school? Did it want me to join those millions of dupes who put their whole hope of life into a story of a zombie Jew?

Every year, they tried to shove it down our throats. "Keep Christ in Christmas." "There's a war on Christmas." There was that outrage over the stupid coffee cups a couple years ago. There were the sanctimonious lawn displays of nativity scenes, as if their dead grass in the middle of winter is somehow holier than the nextdoor neighbor with a Grinch stealing the lights.

That damn imp wanted me to say *that* was the reason for Christmas?

No.

I wasn't going to do it. It couldn't be the answer. I would *not* say that was true, no matter what this thing wanted me to say.

I stared at the creature as it waited for my response with a grin on its lips, as if it knew what I was thinking. I could see it waiting for me to give the Jesus answer, the only one that remained. Would it laugh and cackle at the ridiculous answer? Was that the whole joke? Or was the joke that I was missing something? Despite what it said, it felt as if this were a trick question.

It tilted its head and raised its eyebrows, as if to say, "I'm waiting."

Fine. I couldn't hold out forever.

"The reason for Christmas," I said, "is that people were depressed because of the lack of sunlight in winter so they made up a myth about God becoming man."

The imp's smile widened to cover its whole face. Horror and despair flooded my chest. "Do you know," it asked slowly, "if someone can die from lack of sleep? Let's test it."

NINE

aeternitas

ELIZABETH RUDA

TO THE PARSON *of the county of Whiltmore, or his Secretary.*

I write on behalf of my widower grandfather, who I believe was once one of your congregation. His age has caught up with his spirit, and he is of the fear that he will soon be left hollow and grey in the dead of night. Apologies for my lack of circumlocution, but I see little purpose in discretion, as our family has been called in to discuss his final effects. On taking stock of his remaining estate, we have discovered various papers, books of prayer, and other such items that indicate a prior and committed attendance at St. Mary's. I prefer not to inconvenience you before the holiday, but an aunt has requested your speedy arrival at Barcom House, Dartmoor, Devonshire, with the appropriate oil, instruments, etc. so as to facilitate his rest; I am unfamiliar with your rites. We are willing to cover fees if required, and can provide lodging, as the drive will undoubtedly require it in this unusually severe weather.

If that is reason enough to draw you away from your duties, then you may stop reading here, though this aunt of mine, respected in her various circles, has suggested you and your office take a particular interest in curious and unexplainable affairs. As such, she has resolved I should tell you the entire tale as I have heard it.

She would write herself, had she not thrown her entire being into nursing the poor man—if his every groan and complaint were not at least somewhat exaggerated, the man should have died twenty times over by this point. Still, I know he is indeed not long for this world. He is barely able to rise from bed, with such tremors and shakes so as to make daily life impossible. I assist my aunt where I am able—we await the rest of the family's arrival, gathering for one last time in these old halls. The snow sorely delays them, and I hope you are not met with the same trouble. In the meantime, I continue to organise my grandfather's affairs and mind my aunt's son, my young cousin.

In any case, I regret to note the following narrative is true, inasmuch as I have accurately received and documented it, and that its effects on my family's interests grow unavoidably obvious. In your patience, I hope you shall consider the facts as I shall describe them, though if you are unable to provide commentary or advice on this matter, in lieu of sending us all to be committed, perhaps it may serve as appropriate entertainment for your congregation at Christ's Mass (given the names involved to be anonymized).

Firstly, I must introduce myself. I am James Verney, the son of a merchant, who was himself the same. My grandfather amassed a veritable fortune from the rollicking spice trade of India and its isles. It was not long before my grandfather returned home honourably and with coffers to show for it, and soon found a bride in my late grandmother, Beatrice. She was of great solace to him in his trials, and he to her after a falling out with her own relations. It was their wedding portrait that first turned our attention to St. Mary's, though I believe he stopped attending upon her sudden fate. At least that is as far as his chequebook indicates—though I am getting ahead of myself.

I am some flavour of a tardy Romantic, I fear, and as such am used to frustrating my relations with flights of fancy. I devoured their writings alongside my studies at Oxford, and I tend to preach that I was born too late to walk among such greats. Yet on the whole, my attention lingers in the present, particularly in the books I balance for my father, and I care little for convention's weight. I trust you have already found me somewhat irritating, but I again beg your patience, as well as my own, for the sake of my forebears' devotion.

Now, it is to my misfortune that I did not know my grandmother well. I remember fondly holidays out to their summer home by the sea, with she and my mother and aunt walking us along the tide pools, teaching us of all the glories of Creation. I recall one instance in which I had asked whether the sea cucumbers should be gathered in for lunch—her merry laugh was like bells, her embrace like the hearth, her face all but glowing in the rays of the overhead sun. I did not understand why it was humorous at the time, but she thanked me for my eagerness and bade me help prepare the ones that she'd grown in the garden. My grandmother was glad to take matters into her own hands, often rising earlier than the maid herself, and her hands guided mine at the board and with the knife. My assistance in the kitchen became somewhat of an annual tradition, then a reliance when I visited, as the whole of my relatives came less and less and her vision became darker, dimmer, and more opaque. It was one of those things doctors could not remedy, despite all their wealth. Grandfather immediately took up the tasks of caring for her. I recall going to get a glass of water in what I thought was the middle of the night and restraining a shriek at his ghastly face in the corridor; he rose earlier than even her each day to fetch her beloved lemon balm tea.

One December night some fifteen years ago, he rose, came to wake her with the cup and saucer, and dropped them at the piercing sound of her cry. It was a sound so loud and desperate that the maid (who now tells me this story) believed my grandmother was being torn in two. He dashed into the room, but saw no one; the furniture stood as normal, and the window was closed. Grandmother's arms grasped wildly at the darkness, and she rasped out, "Martin! Martin!" over and over. She did not calm until my grandfather's hand graced her cheek. Her arms caught him like cords, and she did not let go even when the servants wished to check her for wounds. (The maid continued to listen at the door.) Finally she allowed him to sit back down on the bed, though he still gripped her hand, a rock in the candlelight. Before he could even ask, she spoke:

"My brother—I saw him."

This gave the man a start. "Your brother?"

"He says I shall see him soon."

"He is not here, my dear. No one but us."

"He walked along the foot of the bed. He was in agony, the flames licking up his face—"

He pulled her in close. "This questioning again? You know you were not responsible for his tepidity."

"I—I know, James, but I must pray things went well—that he came to see the truth—"

"Please, my love. You will do no good meditating on nightmares."

Here she, as I am told, looked him directly in the eye.

"I was awake."

Nine days later, she passed. It was Christmas Eve.

This brother of hers was a relative neither I nor my cousins had ever met, and whose funeral my aunt only vaguely remembers. It was a challenge for us to even recall his name, let alone any strange nightly trips made to Barcom House, and I cannot find mention of him in my research. I lightly questioned my grandfather about him, and he would not give any response whatsoever. My aunt claims he cannot hear. I often question if he wants to.

At her death, the house became quiet. The servants, even years later, hardly dared speak above a whisper. (Perhaps this is why he is now hard of hearing.) But the stories did not stop.

A visitor was gearing up his horse at the end of the holidays, bidding Grandfather and my parents goodbye, when the harness for his carriage decided to act as though it had not been fastened and checked twice. The horse broke free, fleeing into the wilderness beyond the grounds. An attempt was made to follow the prints. Not long into the search, a violent, icy storm broke out, and the party had little choice but to scramble back to the house. Yet a few hours later, standing outside the front gates, and fastened to a now inexplicably singed harness, was the horse, without any sign of fear or injury. It was retold for years afterward that had the visitor left when he originally intended, he would have been caught in the storm and perished on the way—the road to Barcom is long, with little to shelter a traveller.

Yet another story involves my young cousin. Lawrence, a tender harbinger of mischief, was told to not play too close to the fire, lest he become too directly like his namesake. He ran to and fro between the tree and the fireplace, the bright baubles and wondrous gifts dancing in his eyes, and his hands trailed quite near the grate as he wandered. As was and is his tendency, he did not listen, and lost his footing. He stumbled toward the grate, but before his hands could be seared to its surface, he suddenly stopped inches above it, suspended in midair, nothing visible supporting him. His mother hurried over, scooping him into her arms. Only then did he begin to cry in fright, pointing not at the fire, but at the empty wall beside it.

I should like to chalk such things up to coincidence, happenstance, overactive imaginations, or even the tricks of coarser servants filling our dreams with brimstone and wailing. Yet I myself heard, while the others were at service, my name whispered in the dark of night; I saw the pages of my book unfurled like sails caught at sea. I abandoned my reading and looked for an open window or some other source of draft, but, as you may guess, found none. All I found, when I turned back to my chair, was a dark, ashen smudge like the shape of a hand seemingly burned into the last page. Perhaps it had been there previously, the result of some mishap by candlelight. Perhaps it had not. If not, and I was merely drunk on too much Christmas wine, well, I suppose our lives shall continue, though I will be left to wonder, perhaps chuckle at the strangeness that is life in this world. Your interest and commentary on these matters are encouraged, though if you find none for us, your service to my grandfather will nevertheless be deeply, deeply appreciated.

I leave you, and await your arrival,
   James V.

~

Father White's fingers had stiffened at the very notion of going out in this cold. And on Christmas Eve, too, by the time the letter had come late the night of the 23rd. He kept them squarely in his pockets the entire ride to Dartmoor. But really, he thought, his forebears had walked this road in sandals, more likely than not. He had a carriage. And if this did not work out, if the young man was nothing more than a drunkard and a scoffer and the house full of hot air, well, at least someone had known to reach out, and the old man's soul would be preserved. Or so he hoped.

Gratitude, old man, he chided himself. *Gratitude.*

The driver himself was in a sorrier state. Snow piled atop his hat, his ears red with chill. It had taken a good deal of time for Father White to find anyone still roaming the streets at this hour, and though he assumed necessity (as was his own case), he wondered what could bring a man to take up work the night of the Lord's birth. He knocked on the carriage's wall, putting on his best though unconvincing attempt at a smile, and inquired after his family, what would be for supper on the coming feast. The driver's head turned slightly toward him as he spoke, but there was no response, save the hoofbeats continually stomping a new path into the solid blank.

Father White crumpled back down into his seat, his sigh curling over the top of his coat. *I should be grateful he sent a driver at all.*

After a while longer, the carriage stopped with a jerk—he alighted, and after an extended self-argument, ended up tipping the man rather well.

"Thank you once again. I do hope this isn't too far for you... though I suppose you and your horse would not have taken it if it were, hm?"

The priest never knew a man's eyes to look so lost. The driver simply turned and drove off, without a word.

The priest huffed, more steam puffing up through his scarf. *A happy Christmas to you too.* He stood there for some time, watching the carriage's lantern be swallowed up by the night, but could not wait after him for much longer. "Mr. Verney" had need of him. And his fingertips were beginning to freeze.

His grumbling had held a bit of truth: the way to Barcom House from Whiltmore was considerably arduous, with rocks and crags invisible under the still falling snow. It was not extremely far from his usual jurisdiction, but even then, and despite the size of its grounds, he had never heard of it. Perhaps the previous pastor knew the couple; Father White had only come in the last seven years or so. But even then.

The wind ripped into him. His hands broke free from their pockets as he rubbed them vigorously together for warmth and blew in between them. He continued uphill, but the path went on longer, and he could not yet see the house. A few minutes more, and he began to wonder if this was the way to Barcom at all. He whispered into his hands, praying he would keep them even if he collapsed there on the lawn. Then, as if in reply, light broke through the flurry. An open door shone through the storm, high overhead, unwavering.

A bit further, and Father White crossed into the house.

"Dear me," cried the maid, shuddering behind the massive door as he stomped the snow off his boots. "You look like death incarnate, all in black like that."

"I surely hope not, madam," he replied. "I take it I have beaten him here?"

"Yes, though barely. I take it the letter came later than we'd hoped," said a man at the top of a large mahogany staircase. He was wiry, dressed in a suit too light for the season, and puffed at a small pipe in hand, with the other in his pants pocket. He hurried down as the maid shoved herself against the door—by its size, her entire weight was needed to shut it. As it closed, a rumble echoed all down the halls. The grandson had a businessman's grip, and the priest guessed him to be somewhere in his mid twenties, as a hint of freckle remained visible on his cheeks.

"So glad you could come. He had a slight scare a few moments ago, and we are all awake, except for Lawrence. I do hope it was not more trouble than usual."

Father White cocked an eyebrow. "You are quite the honest fellow, aren't you?"

Mr. Verney laughed heartily. (He did not smell of drink.) "In all the drama we endure in life, Reverend, it is my duty to say things as they are." He led the priest up the stair.

"Do you find death a drama?"

"This one certainly is," he replied, shaking his head. "Come, I do not wish to waste too much of your time."

Father White grabbed his sleeve, and the man stopped, turning to him. "I am not in the business of rushing sacraments, lad."

Mr. Verney smiled. "Apologies. As you wish." At a markedly slower pace, seemingly against his natural gait, he continued up the stair.

Strange boy, thought the priest, thinking back to his description of the unction in the letter. It had been apparent he knew little of the rite's meaning, and likely cared less for religion itself, but surely he had witnessed it with his late grandmother, or some other relative, and knew what it entailed?

He came into the master bedroom. A woman with dark hair sat beside the four-poster bed, clasping the withered hand of its occupant within her own flushed two. The gaunt, pale, and irrepressibly old man's eyes were closed, and he was encircled by enough pillows and blankets so as to resemble a child. She looked on him with tired, moist eyes.

Mr. Verney the grandson gave a quiet cough. "Is he—?"

"Oh!" whispered the woman, rising and laying the hand on the man's lap, despite Father White's insistence for her to remain seated. She came and greeted him warmly. "You are the priest!"

"I am the priest," he replied, softening somewhat. *O Lord, rebuke my pride.*

"He is just resting a moment—a terrible nightmare, I believe. He said something of having heard voices, and awoke with a scream."

"And so woke the rest of us," the grandson grumbled. The woman shot him a look, and he went back to smoking his pipe.

"I can wake him for you, unless you'd rather wait til morning."

"No, no, I think now would be best," said Father White. "I've heard a little of your family's history, and I do not wish to prolong anxieties."

"Thank you ever so much." She immediately turned back to the old man.

"What is your name, madam?"

"Me? Oh," she exclaimed, blinking. "My name is Veronica. My father is James, and I believe you have met my nephew."

The priest smiled ever so slightly and bowed his head. Aunt Veronica leaned in and spoke into her father's ear.

"Father? Father. The pastor of St. Mary's is here. Yes, for you! Yes, for confession."

The old man opened one dark eye. "What popery do you bring to this house?" he slurred.

The three froze.

"The shameless kind, my dear sir," Father White finally mused. "Though from what I understand, you possess a good deal of it yourself, or did, at one time."

The man rolled over and buried his face in the covers. Veronica shook his shoulder, voice warbling through her smile. "Father, please, he has come all this way, and you know it is important—"

"Go away! Go away!" he groaned, swatting at her. She pulled away, and the grandson came to her side, squinting.

"Well, isn't this something," he said, dryly.

Why yes, son. It indeed is something. Some wretched waste of my time. Surely you were the top of your class! Oh...hush.

Father White sucked in a breath, and he gathered his hat and bag. "If it is no great trouble for the both of you, I believe this conversation should wait for the morning after all."

"No trouble at all," the young man replied.

The woman was in mild shock. "Please forgive me; I did not—"

Father White shook his head, suppressing his ire. "He is likely still half asleep, and hardly knows what he is saying. Let us rest, and be refreshed in the Lord's good time."

The relatives looked at each other, and Veronica frowned, but nodded.

The light was put out, and all went to bed. A room had been prepared for Father White as promised, and after night prayer, he soon went to sleep. It was not long before he felt he was not alone.

A dream came to him, one of shadows, swirling like ink across the page of the garden. They grew into the forms of people, men, women, children—faceless, grey, and ashen. Whispers filled the air as though rain; weeping followed as though a monsoon. The snow melted where they stepped.

Please...

The sun finally began to peek around the curtains. Father White reached for his glasses in their place on the nightstand, then remembered it was on the other side, unlike in his own room. He rolled over to grab them.

A crashing and banging drove him into the headboard.

"Good morning!" called the grandson through the door. "He is awake now, if you are! My aunt is making tea." His steps then continued down the hall.

Father White rubbed his head. This was all too much. The tales had begun to influence him. His need was to remain objective, to provide comfort. And yet...and yet. Father White stepped over to the window, peering at the solid white garden below.

In the master bedroom, the old man lay with his face toward the wall, his thin body still swallowed by the bedding. The young Mr. Verney puffed away at the window.

"Ah, Grandfather, the reverend has come to see you."

The man blinked, but remained sullen.

Father White set his bag on the dresser. "I suppose his hearing has gotten worse overnight."

"Only for anyone who is not my aunt," the young man replied, shaking his head.

Father White sat down in the chair beside the bed, his anointing kit on his lap, and placed a hand on the elder man's arm. "If you please," he said to the other, nodding toward the door. The grandson glanced again at the bed, sighed, and left, shutting the door.

Father White leaned in closer. "Sir, I have come quite a ways to—"

The man brushed off his touch. "I am sorry for your trouble, but I still have nothing to say to God, nor to any man who comes in His stead."

The priest blinked, then blinked again. "Mr. Verney—"

"It has been that way for many years."

"And do you wish it to be so unto eternity?" he asked, incredulous.

The man said nothing. There was a long pause between them, only broken by a sputtering cough. Father White leaned in again, begging pleasure to overtake the anger boiling up in his throat.

"Mr. Verney, I do not wish to irritate you. I wish to help you. If this is in regards to—" There was murmuring at the door, then a knock. "A moment, if you please."

Yet it was the old man's tea, and the old man bade them come anyway. (Father White sighed, rubbing his eyelids). Veronica entered and began to distribute the cups and saucers to each of them, with her nephew at her heels. The priest was grateful for his steaming cup, having missed breakfast, albeit was disgruntled at the fact that it had to be here, now, in this room at all. He gave the lady his seat, and she held her father's cup to his lips, his own hands shaking in the attempt to receive it. One cup remained on the tray, growing cold. The grandson gave a look to the priest, who only gazed at his elder, thinking. A spray erupted from the old man's mouth.

"Gah—what is this? Lemon balm? Is this some sort of joke?"

Veronica's face went as pale as the lawn, and she glanced fearfully at the other two. "No, it's your Earl Grey...same as always, Father. There is no lemon in it."

He shoved the cup away, its tea splashing onto her skin. She grimaced, but lowered her head to sniff its contents. Her eyes widened. She held the cup by the tips of her fingers and turned to her nephew. He set down his own cup, stuffed a hand in one pocket, and took the new cup with the other. One quick, loud slurp—his eyebrows furrowed, and he nodded. He passed it, finally, to the priest. It indeed smelled of lemon. There was no denying it. But the rest of the cups contained Earl Grey.

"There has been no lemon balm in the house for the better part of... twenty years, I'd say," Veronica mumbled. "Not since—"

"O, to torment an old man in his last days!" the old man cried, and descended into unintelligible groaning, burying his face into his blankets.

The lady held a hand over her mouth. The priest looked into the cup.

"Mr. Verney... excuse me. Where is your wife buried?"

The family blinked at him. The man only ground his teeth, muttering still.

"Under the willow in the garden," the grandson answered, half shrugging. "Why?"

"Was any clergy involved in her burial? Anyone to pray?"

He scratched his cheek. "Well, it was during a snowstorm—not unlike this one, I'm afraid, and didn't let up for days after. Grandfather, did you send for a clergyman once she was—"

"No."

A spark shot across Father White's eyes like a bullet grazing the surface of a still pond.

The grandson looked back at him. "Is...there a problem?"

"There is a problem indeed, and has been for some time."

~

"I did not—I did not realise—" cried Veronica, shivering in her coat. Those present and able had gathered under the willow tree, per Father White's command.

He flipped through his book of prayer. "Were you not here when it happened?"

"We were to come for the holiday, but Father did not allow visitors for weeks after. I had no question he took care of things in the meanwhile..."

"Surely you must have known *something* was amiss," he said. She shook her head.

"His devotion was true. He had converted to the faith when they were to be married, and loved her with all his heart—I am sorry he was so rude to your office. He was, and still must be, heartbroken, even unto the Lord Himself."

"Do you call that devotion?" he almost snapped.

Veronica thought for a moment. Tears began spilling down her cheeks. "To her. But it was not right. It is not right."

Father White frowned deeply, and looked at his feet. "I am sorry."

Her tears glistened in the sun.

"I felt a need to ask, given the irregularities seen here. But you know what this means. I shall not berate you any further. I have what I need to set things right—Beatrice will soon be at peace. In any case, these were your father's decisions, not yours. I do not hold them against you. I pray he has a change of heart, and comes to know what you do, before it is too late."

"If I may interject," said Mr. Verney, and their eyes shifted to him, "I do not quite see what the big deal is if she is here or in some cemetery miles away. She is in the ground one way or another."

"James!" Veronica hissed.

Father White's nostrils flared. "Lad, you do not know what you take so lightly, what you continually belittle. It is eternity we contend with. This life will be a whisper by comparison, a puff of smoke."

Mr. Verney glanced at his pipe.

"I am no bishop, nor exorcist, so I cannot make a formal declaration, but the events you have described greatly recall the purgation given to those souls granted Heaven, but still bear imperfections to be remedied in death. They are cleansed by holy fire, and cannot escape it except in two ways: the passage of time, and our charity in prayer."

"That... does not sound rather appealing," he said.

"No, but most of us allowed into Paradise will likely pass through it—if we are granted such at all, if the blessed Lord has been allowed to work through us in our time. That is why we offer sacrifice for the dead. With no funeral Mass offered, no anointing given, no consecrated ground for burial, your mother may very well be waiting longer than she would have otherwise. Yet once souls are cleansed, they are freed from their brokenness, and we find no more pain within, finding instead rest in the bosom of our Creator, who loves us without end."

"But why all the anguish? The strange happenings and signs? Can they not simply ask us to pray?"

"That is how they ask. They are simply making sure you pay attention."

The snow had slowed and stopped that morning just as the group had come to the garden, and all around them, the remaining white sparkled, as though a shroud strewn with diamonds. The resulting brilliance was blinding; the grandson shifted occasionally, wishing to return inside. Yet with Father White there, a black column struck in its centre, James Verney could not look away. None of them could. The giant, dark arrow pointed to something hidden in the silence. Then his voice rang out across the snow's surface, calling to those bones in wait beneath: "*In nomine Patris, et Filii, et Spiritus Sancti...*"

As the rite continued, the priest sighed inside. *Lord, have pity on me, so disgruntled and so hard of heart. Make me like Yourself, like those I have met in this place who love with all they have. Yet guide us in right paths, for Your Name's sake.* He took up a hymn in closing, raising his eyes toward the tree, and saw a dark-clad woman standing beside it, her dress and hands wreathed in smoke. His voice caught in his throat; the woman smiled. She—along with a host of others like her—joined in the song.

Deaf ears hear the silent tongues
sing away their weeping;
Blind eyes see the lifeless ones
walking, running, leaping.

As it ended, and his book shut, they disappeared, the grass now visible where they had stood. James looked up from his thoughts—his pipe landed in the snow.

When Father White came to the old man's room again, he swore he could just make out a voice—

"Yes, my dear. I will. I promise. I will go to Him! I will see you!"

The man was sitting upright, hand outstretched, as if holding the hand of another. He looked to the priest, tears in his eyes.

That hour, Father White heard his last confession.

It was Christmas Eve.

about the authors

Listed in order of appearance

Jessica McKendry's primary claim to fame (and the one that she usually drops as a sort of conversational bomb at parties) lies in being the eldest of twelve children. A big family has definite perks: your siblings become your best friends and there are always babies around to cuddle! When she isn't embarking on a random niche hobby, Jessica fills her time with art, books, music, and historical documentaries.

E.B Grimm spent a number of years as an accountant in the Shenandoah before moving to New England to pursue higher education. While this is her first time being published, she has moonlighted as a writer, especially a writer of all things grim and hopeful, through many years of life changes. When she is not writing or studying, she can be found listening to folk music, in Adoration, or in a graveyard.

Grace F. Hopkins is an editor, ghost writer, (who also writes the occasional ghost story) and co-founder of Inkwells & Anvils. Her short fiction has appeared in "The Crow's Quill" and "Legend Fiction" anthologies. Her poetry has been published with Knee Brace Press. She flavors her fiction with the eldritch & transcendental and Tweets about writing @graceswritesalt.

Madeline Shepley is a planetarium director and physics/astronomy professor who moonlights as a faith-inspired sci-fi author in her spare time. She is a Hoosier, bred and educated, where she first developed a passionate love of astronomy, reading, and writing. When not delving into stories or stargazing, you might find her podcasting, cheering on her favorite sports teams, or plotting her next international excursion.

Zephyr Thomas writes about ordinary people doing extraordinary things, as well as extraordinary people doing ordinary things. He also writes stories about taming magical creatures in the modern day and on the wild frontier. Like gardening, he knows that it takes time for the best stories to ripen properly. Find him at zmthomas.com

Ben Stapleton is an aspiring author who mostly writes short stories. He's trying his hand at writing full length novels, and primarily writes in the fantasy and science-fiction genres. By day he sunlights as an electrical engineer and by night can be found painting miniatures, reading, or writing.

Kelly Gross is one of the co-founders of Inkwells & Anvils and this is her first official published work. During the day, she works as an accountant and at night she explores fictional worlds while taking care of her goldendoodle.

E.P. Fuselier is the founder of Wordsmiths—precursor to Inkwells & Anvils—an idea that came to her when she wanted to grow in her craft of writing alongside other Catholic authors. She loves writing fantasy but enjoys all sorts of genres— fantasy, sci-fi, historical non-fiction, biographies. She hates cliches but still says her favorite authors are J.R.R. Tolkien, C.S. Lewis, and Jane Austen.

ELIZABETH RUDA is an editor, author, and artist based in Saint Louis, Missouri. With one foot in fantasy and the other in sci-fi, she works to bring the Church's truth, beauty, and goodness to an aching world. She can be found on LinkedIn.

INKWELLS & ANVILS is a community for Catholic Storytellers founded in January of 2023 by eight writers looking to provide a space for creatives with shared values. Inspired by the writing group of the Inklings themselves, I&A fosters growth in craft, character, and appreciation of the good, true, and beautiful. Become part of Inkwells & Anvils by following them on social media, checking out their website (inkwellsandanvils.com), or joining their Discord Server (see their website for how to) today.

X x.com/InkwellsAnvils
instagram.com/inkwellsanvils

acknowledgments

First and foremost we would like to thank God, in whose Great and Good creation we are mere subcreators. Second is Catherine the All Seeing Eye (well, most seeing), who took the initiative to bring this project to fruition. Next is the Risking Enchantment podcast, who gave the inspiration to E. P. Fuselier for a Christmas ghost story anthology. We thank Grace Malinee and Paige Guerra for their diligent editing, along with Ben, E. P., and Kelly who acted as judges and editorial collaborators. We would also like to thank all who submitted stories for this Anthology, especially our five contributors Elizabeth, Grimm, Jessica, Madeline, and Zephyr.

More widely, we would like to thank all of the Wordsmiths who founded such a vibrant writing community as Inkwells & Anvils. We've already thanked Catherine, E. P. Fuselier, Grace, Paige, and Kelly so we'll extend it to Lauren, Robert, and Tyler.

In no particular order we also thank Leanne, Carah, Samantha-wise, Bob who is a Squire, Fr Don Siple, Danielle W, and Jake for their invaluable feedback on the works contained herein.

We also owe a huge wealth of gratitude to the people that choose to write and storytell every day, especially those in the Inkwells & Anvils community who, by just their presence and enthusiasm, help make things like this a joy to put together.

Finally and most importantly we'd like to thank you, the reader. Because a story doesn't really live until someone reads it, until someone like you lets the pages breathe and enter your imagination. **Thank you!**